DECADENCE KILLS

Michael P. Charlton

CHAPTER 1

I sit on the edge of our bed, rocking back and forth like a maniac in an insane asylum, Mrs. Sykes beside me. I press her clammy hands and she brushes our dry, scabby feet against each other. We romantically rub our fingers and click toes at the same time. Horny hand massages and flexible foot aerobics. We both want to hold onto this precious moment for as long as possible. This is the most incredible day of our pointless lives. We are changing the grey clouds which hang over our heads into bright, sparkling, rainbow disco flickers.

Mrs. Sykes softly looks into my watery eyes. The romance makes me slightly uncomfortable. It's unusual for us to be like this. Usually, it's a case of amicably barging past each other in the morning and separately going about our days. You've got to work at life. Nothing good comes naturally. That's what Mrs. Sykes always says. We have to work at love. Every day there will be a new argument that has to be resolved. Both having to talk things through after a screaming match the night before. But we never spend the entire day angry at each other.

Mrs. Sykes whines out tears of joy!

She manages to trigger my emotions. We've always allowed the other to feel and to love, but I could never cope with the consequences which came with it. I let it all out. Years of emotional suppression, pretending that nothing mattered, and holding everything inside when it most needed to come out.

Mrs. Sykes grabs my head and thrusts it into her chest. She lightly strokes my hair with the tips of her fingers. I feel like she's ripped off my phallus, torn it to pieces, and shoved it up my ass. Within minutes of revealing my vulnerability, I can sense a tiny dash of her respect for me has fluttered out of the window, like a butterfly with a damaged wing.

"I can't believe he did it. I mean, wow, he actually did it."

"Yes, he did."

"How?"

I push myself up to answer Mrs. Sykes' question. A sense of relief glazes out of her sockets as it's confirmed that she doesn't need to hold a crying weasel.

"Who cares how he did it."

"It's just, like, it's crazy."

I gently touch Mrs. Sykes' warm, rosy red cheeks. She aggressively pushes my hand away and quickly turns her back on me. Mrs. Sykes confidently stands up. I sit up straight on the edge of our bed and stare at her enormous baby bump! I watch her rub, stroke, and tickle her massive pregnant belly.

"You don't expect this to happen, do you? This isn't meant to be real. I'm still not sure that any of this is."

"I promise this is real."

"I'm expecting to wake up. The alarm will go off any minute, or you'll nudge me to stop snoring, or I'll need to take a piss. Something will wake me up, and this will all be a dream. Because I've dreamt about this happening for years."

"Now it has."

"We need to do something."

"Like what, darl?"

"Loads of pregnancy tests."

"Does an enormous baby bump not say it all?"

"No!"

Mrs. Sykes is trying to wrap her head around this insane event, waking up nine months pregnant and ready to drop with a newborn.

"Mr. P has clearly come through for us."

"I guess, err, well, yeah, he must have..."

"There's no other way you could be this level of pregnant overnight."

"Hmm."

Mrs. Sykes trails around our bedroom with her hair tightly plaited into pigtails. Each pigtail flip-flops and bounces side to side as she picks up the pace of walking around the room. Her cheeks have gone bright red from the overwhelming excitement. The next step will be for Mrs. Sykes to pull out her pigtails and bring her curls to life while putting some slap on her face to calm down the Rosacea.

We couldn't have kids. Well, she couldn't have kids. We've tried. Medication, scans, surrogates, you name it. Mrs. Sykes has spent years fighting through bursts of panic and anxiety. She said the pains felt tremendously uncomfortable and sharp, with agonising heart palpitations. The sensations leave her body and fly away like a dark, vicious crow that haunts her nightmares.

Mrs. Sykes' ovaries are so dried up that scorpions could run around. A tossup between the Australian outback and Sahara Dessert. These are Mrs. Sykes' jokes, not mine. I'm merely the special counsel to my wife's sterile hilarity. Up until this point, the likelihood of her getting preggers was pretty much zero percent. Her uterus and womb have been as useless as a rocket built to compete against the speed of light. It just wasn't ever going to happen.

Mrs. Sykes slowly removes her pink dressing gown, which drops and spreads across our carpet. Now she's completely naked. Her pregnant belly pushes over her toes. She turns to me and points in child-like amusement.

"This is unbelievable. Look at me! I can't even see my feet."

Mrs. Sykes tramples around the bedroom, knocking into ornaments and photo frames. She jiggles her bum and giggles, shakes her boobs and squeaks, strokes her belly, and weeps. A hyper-excited mixture of confusion and joy.

"Imagine the milk that will squirt out of these..."

Mrs Sykes stands over me and squeezes her boobs. She pretends to be a cow who is squirting milk into my mouth.

"Moo! Moo! Moo! I want to feed you. Put this on your Coco Pops, Mr. Sykes?"

"It's incredible, darl."

"Is this a ridiculously vivid dream?"

"Stop saying that. You're annoying me now. All the evidence points to it being real. Well, I guess it depends on what you mean by real. Anyways, err, regardless, we need to stop caring about how this happened. Just accept that it has. Mr. P came through for us. It's clearly a miracle. Miracles have happened since tribes and civilizations were formed. Books and scriptures, myths and tales, over millions of years, all talk about miracles.

This is one of them. The baby could be, y'know, it could be God? This could be the next Jesus? Oh! Or, you're the new Virgin Mary?"

"I don't think so."

"It could easily be."

"Don't use the lord's name in vain."

"Maybe you'll give birth to the anti-Christ?"

Mrs. Sykes cups her hand and slaps me hard behind my left ear.

"Argh! Bitch, that bloody hurt."

"Don't say such horrible things about our baby. Next time you'll get worse than a clip around the ear."

"I'm sorry, you're right, I'm sorry."

"Let's stop talking about Gods and the anti-Christ. It's bad luck. It's making me feel weird."

"As far as I'm concerned, Mr. P has done his job. He told me that he would do this for us. He's done it. Let's accept that we're having a baby."

"Tell me the story again."

"Mr Pyjamas?"

"Yeah. One of my favourites."

"It's hardly the Mahābhāratam."

"I don't know or care what that means, Mr. Sykes."

"Well, err, alright, fine."

"I love this story!"

"Err, well, it was at the shit hole Church before the wake."

A naked Mrs. Sykes lies on the bed with her legs wide open. This is my first time seeing her fully nude with her legs spread in at least a year.

"Err, and then, err, shit, where was I?"

"Too busy staring at my trimmings?"

"Well, yeah, I was."

"It's been a long time."

"It has."

I pace around the room while Mrs. Sykes lies across the bed and watches me. She relaxes and spreads herself. I've not touched that thing in a very long time. I seriously doubt I'd know what to do.

Mrs. Sykes excitedly claps her hands together.

"I pull up to the Church by myself. You lot were all making your way together. I couldn't be arsed to drive across town to go with everybody else."

"I thought you were a selfish twat for doing that."

"I know you did. I've still got the texts."

"Keep going."

"I pull up earlier than everybody else. I drive past the Church, looking for a place to park and expecting to see a huge Gothic cathedral. A Church with an epic Faustian spirit. I'd heard everybody describe it as such. Or, at the very least, all of my lot had said that it looked like a classical building, as much as they could in their slow hillbilly drawls, the kind from medieval England.

But instead, it's this pile of human excrement with the cheek to call itself a house of God. I don't know what the hell this is meant to be. I park around the corner and make my way back to the Church. Loads of rude ignoramuses bumped into me constantly, and shoulder barges violently knocked my body over to one side with no apologies or acknowledgment. I make my way through the crowds of assholes. The building isn't the eye-watering architecture that I was guaranteed. Not at all. It's a shite-fest. Our families have wasted a funeral. I looked up, and the roof tiles were broken, which meant there was likely a leak and water dripping into the building. It's brown and soggy. I decided to give it a chance. It may still be a metaphysical paradise inside. It will definitely be artistic. I try the main doors, and they're locked. So much for a funeral. Who chose this place? I walk down a dirty alleyway through broken glass, used needles, sloshy mud, the stench of poo, and the taste of piss into this crammed sideway door with thick silver chains wrapped around the giant handle. I force my way through the unlocked door. I push past an old, dusty black curtain into this tiny, clownish room."

"What happened next?"

"That's when I saw him. To my left is Mr. Pyjamas. He speaks in an incredibly thick New York accent. He babbles like a wannabee Italian American who has just been cut and pasted from a film, allowed to run wild and free in the real world. He was more attractive than Tony

Soprano but looked equally as psychopathic. Mr. Pyjamas is wearing mostly leather. Leather biker jacket. Leather trousers. Leather belt. Leather dog collar. Leather gloves. Leather boots. Black T-shirt. Black socks. Black sunglasses. He's got his jacket sleeves rolled up and smoking a fag. The packet of cigarettes poking out of his leather jacket pocket. He's got jet-black hair, the blackest I've ever seen, into this enormous quiff. The quiff is gelled and combed at least a couple of inches over his head. Occasionally, he whips the black comb from his pocket and brushes his quiff backward like a maniac. He forcefully and aggressively combs through the waves of hair product dripping from the tips of the comb. After he's finished, he acts calm and collected, propping up his shoulders and clicking his fingers at me like he's Fonzie. Mr. Pyjamas finishes smoking his cigarette. He's filled the room with clouds of smoke that smell like an unwashed car garage. I cough and cough and cough until finally, Mr. Pyjamas stands up. He's huge! A lot taller than I expect him to be. I hear his leather jacket stretching and his leather trousers rip. We both pretend that it didn't happen. Mr. Pyjamas combs his hair again, and again, and again. He lights another cigarette and returns to his seat."

"What did he say? Did he speak to you?"

"Yeah, he spoke to me. In hindsight, he's a strange beast, but I'm a weirdo too, so who cares. After introducing himself and telling me his name, he started chatting me up first."

Mrs. Sykes leans against the headboard as I tell her what has been said.

"Kid?"

"Yes?"

"Mind if I light up, again?"

"Go for it. Just out of interest, how old are you?"

"How old do you want me to be, kid?"

"Err, well, just tell me your actual age."

"I'm eighteen, yeah, that's the one, eighteen."

I sit at the foot of the bed and move closer to Mrs. Sykes. She has a big grin like I'm a male stripper at an old lady's retirement party.

"There's no chance in hell that he's eighteen. He's got old man forehead lines and past-his-prime face wrinkles. He looks about forty. I'm guessing the old git is in his forties. I nod and grin at Mr. Pyjamas. I'm not crumbling first. He's going to have to collapse and admit he's lying. I'm not confronting him. We continue talking about his age."

"You're eighteen, wow!"

"What, kid?"

"That is the perfect age, my good man. The best age. Eighteen is the age we all want to get to when we're young. When we can drink, smoke, shag, gamble, vote, the list goes on and on. We'd kill to reach eighteen quicker when we're kids. But eighteen is also the age

that we all wish we still were. The age we have emotional nostalgia for. Memories that we take with us to our graves are the best memories. Music, travelling, activities, dreams. We would all kill to travel backward and have one more chance at eighteen. But you've still got that special gift, my good man. I'm telling you from experience, enjoy it, fucking enjoy it, mate. Please make the most of every second because you'll never get it back. You won't be able to do any of it again. Before you know it, you'll be thirty, like me. Crying in toilets and watching old hags die in your arms."

"That means a lot. Thanks, kid."

I push myself off the bed and walk around the room.

"That's deep, Mr. Sykes."

"Thanks, Mrs. Sykes. It just came flying straight out of my mouth."

"But you went along with his lie?"

"I was taking the piss."

"Lying in the house of God!"

"God would have found it funny."

"Would he?"

"Why would God invent humour if he didn't want us to use it?"

"You make an excellent point, Mr. Sykes."

"So, err, yeah, I nod to Mr. Pyjamas, and he nods to me. Then, he goes back to smoking and staring out of the window. I assume he must work at the Church. This backroom was such a mess. I didn't question whether a guy dressed head to toe in leather would work there."

"What did you do?"

"By this point, I'm getting creeped out. Maybe he isn't just a normal Priest. I walk out of the room and leave the Church. I can hear my family walking over. The main doors are fully open when they get to me. I walk back inside the Church with my lot, and Mr. P is gone."

"Even the thought of him creeps me out."

"I get back to the gaff, y'know, for the wake. But I'm the one who is late this time. You lot are already inside. I pulled up at the top of the street and could already hear our families partying. I got out of the car, stood in a fucking puddle, punched myself in the leg, and continued walking down the street. I see this bloke in leather across the road! I make it to the house, get through the gates, arrive at the door, and Mr. Pyjamas was stood there. He was waiting for me. We got chatting for quite a while. He started making me all of these promises, saying that he could help us have a baby. I assumed he meant a surrogate or something. I told him we'd already tried it. He assured me that he could make it happen."

After what feels like hours but is more likely minutes, Mrs. Sykes staggers off the bed and shuffles to the bathroom. I can hear the sound of her being sick. I start to get dressed while Mrs. Sykes chucks up her guts.

Eventually, both of our families left and went home last night.

While me and Mrs. Sykes were trying to sleep, they were all still outside, laughing their heads off like a pack of Hyenas and screeching and cackling like a gang of disabled witches falling off their broomsticks. They sounded more like a celebration than a mourning. You could tell they were all hammered because our families spoke in even thicker accents.

They may as well have ripped their ragged clothes from their large bodies and started beating their chests at each other, climbing trees and battling it out for the biggest gammon, flinging shit at each other from the trees. Both of our families scoffed quiche and downed whisky. It sounded like the last days of Rome. It wouldn't surprise me if Mrs. Sykes' mother didn't whip down her lacy knickers, bend over the expensive patio furniture and let all of the men in both of our families stick it up her. One after the other. A competition to see who could rip her apart. She's fifty-seven and has three kids, so it could take a while. But the roughest bang wins a prize. Maybe, another session on her? Or a whole quiche and bottle of whisky to himself. Wow! That would be nice for them, wouldn't it? Keep their small-minded brains interested in something outside their egos for a few minutes.

When I say unbearable, I mean it. Not a single member of our hick families has any social awareness what's so ever. They're trapped in their own little worlds of arrogance and self-importance, which everybody else must adapt to communicate with them. So we have to lower ourselves significantly to have a most basic conversation.

Mrs. Sykes' crazy mother and insane sister got into a big fight in the garden. We were in bed by this point. Mrs. Sykes' insane sister was hammered. She'd drank bottle after bottle of red wine. She had her colossal size E boobs out and began to give her Navy husband a lap dance and a blowjob. Mrs. Sykes' crazy mother tried to convince her insane daughter to put her boobs away, especially in front of Mrs Sykes' old and decerped grandparents. Mrs. Sykes' insane sister punched their crazy mother in the face. She told everybody that her crazy mother used to be a prostitute, that her estranged dad sexually abused her, and that they sent her off to boarding school, where she was allegedly abused. Mrs. Sykes' crazy mother stormed out of the house alongside her boyfriend. Mrs. Sykes' religious auntie tried to speak with the insane sister. The religious auntie wanted to force her to admit it was all a pack of lies. That there was no childhood abuse. Refusing to listen, the religious auntie punched the insane sister in the face, trying to slap some sense into her. At this point, the insane sister put her colossal size E boobs away. The Navy husband, who drank bottle after bottle of wine, at least six-foot-three, stood up and punched the religious auntie in the face! Thankfully, the old grandparents had gone home by this point, then the religious auntie and her husband left. Finally, Mrs. Sykes' insane sister and her Navy husband stumbled off.

After Mrs. Sykes' family had broken down, only my lot was left at our family's wake. My conspiracy uncle was shouting some of his drugged-up flat-earth conspiracy theories. After about an hour of ranting and raving, a few of my family members spoke out. They told him the Earth wasn't flat and that he was just off his head on speed and a complete moron. He went crazy and lost his shit. My conspiracy uncle smashed up the barbecue, screaming at my family, claiming that I was the favourite and nobody had ever loved him. My conspiracy uncle ran out of the house, crying and whining like an obese toddler.

Everybody went home.

Nobody acknowledged that me and Mrs. Sykes were still in the house. I doubt they knew we were still here.

In their eyes, we aren't part of our families if we aren't singing, dancing, screaming, shouting, drinking, and sniffing…

The lives me and Mrs. Sykes used to live were completely different. People around us had fuck all to live for. Neither did we. We'd look out of our windows and see young lads across the road, smoking grass every night. They were twelve or thirteen years old. Their older brothers would be selling dodgy car parts, the size of the dole queues whenever I used to sign on, blokes old enough to be our dad's drinking cans of super-strong beer outside the bookies. Down the road from our old flat, where we used to live would be full of young lasses selling their fucking bodies to pay for their crack habits. The smell of kebabs when you walked down the high street, no one needed a kebab at 11 a.m., but they were still open. There's no need for that smell to be there all of the time, what happened to the smell of fresh air?

It only worsened before we had the good fortune we'd been granted. None of it was improving, despite what those who run things will have you think. This has been going on for as long as we've been around. Everything and everyone is pointless. It isn't all blue sky and freedom, it's grey, and it's hopeless, scary, and fearful, that's what we experienced every time we went outside.

I make my way out of our bedroom and downstairs into the kitchen. Mrs. Sykes' sick is everywhere. It stinks. I look around, and the place is still a dump. Just as bad as outside. All the chairs have holes with all the cotton from the backs dangling onto the seats. There's dust and mould all over the windowsill, and the windows are grafted. They don't look like they've been cleaned in years. The walls are disgusting, dripping in red and yellow crust. The ceiling is black.

I breeze into the front room and sit on the leather sofa. I wait for Mrs. Sykes to stop vomiting. It sounds like she has. She usually needs at least ten minutes to calm down. Destiny has brought us here. Destiny is set in stone by God. The events surrounding it are merely incidental. Everybody hating us, including our screwed-up families, was just a blip in the story which will turn out to be our path to where we were always meant to be. We'll have pushed past the amount of shit, pain, heartbreak, issues, addictions, violence, hatred, abuse, self-harm, loneliness, abandonment…

"Mr. Sykes!"

Mrs. Sykes shouts at me from upstairs.

"Yes, Mrs. Sykes!"

I lean to the side, poke my head around the door and shout back until we communicate like bloody idiots.

"Why did you leave me?"

"You always ask me to leave."

"Not this time."

"Whenever I've tried to stay in the past, you shout at me and say I'm invading your personal space by not letting you have time to yourself. You like being alone when you're sick. You insist on being alone when you're vomiting. You demand to be alone when you're spewing."

"This is different.'"

"I've tried many times, and you always want to be alone."

"That's tablet sickness. This is a different kind of sickness, baby sickness. They're two completely different things. You should know that. Moron! Tablet sickness, I don't need or want anybody near me. Baby sickness, I need and always want you near me. Got it? Oi!"

"Yes."

"Good. Now, come back upstairs."

"I'm relaxing. The gaff and garden need cleaning. Our lot has left everything in a right state. It's disgusting. We're not having them around again, at least not in big groups. I'm so done with our lot. They're animals. Filthy, brain dead, psychotic animals. We'll never need to lend money, need a place to stay, or need help doing up our crappy flat. I'm done with them. My great aunt's inheritance will be the best thing that could have ever happened to us. Her leaving this house to us is a miracle. This is God. Whether we like it or not, no other explanation makes sense than God looking down on us."

"Mr. Sykes?"

"Yes?"

"Have you finished your boring rambling?"

"What?"

"I never asked for your opinion on anything. I told you to get your ass upstairs right now, and what do you choose to do instead? Go on some meaningless rant. I don't give a shit. Stop your blabbering. Clean the house and garden later. Right now, I need you upstairs."

Mrs. Sykes is being harsh. She sounds furious.

"What do you need me for?"

"Just come up here! Stop asking questions."

How can she be so horrible when we're having a baby? I don't like being near her before or after she's sick. She becomes antagonistic and aggressive. Yet, again, Mrs. Sykes tries to smash my phallus into pieces with a rusty hammer.

I peel myself from the sofa and stomp my way upstairs like an angry little brat. That's precisely how Mrs. Sykes has made me feel. I get upstairs and walk past the bathroom. The lights are still on, and the door is open. Yet again, it reeks of her vile vomit. She needs me in the bedroom. Maybe she wants me to shag her? I drag my way up another flight of stairs. I feel like her little servant boy. She's carrying the baby, so I guess this is the part I'll have to play.

"I'm here. This better be good. I was nice and relaxed on that sofa."

I see Mr. Pyjamas.

He's holding a gun to Mrs. Sykes' head.

Her legs are shaking, and she's cowering in fear, trying not to make a sound.

"Mr. P, what, err, what's going on, mate?"

I try to bargain with Mr. Pyjamas and calm down the situation. I'm fired up with anger and trying my best to hide it. I'm attempting to talk Mr. Pyjamas down from the ledge.

"Come on, mate. She's pregnant. Please, just let her go, yeah? Do, err, do whatever you've got to do to me. We can make another deal! How about that?"

"I know she's pregnant, kid. I was the one who made it happen. Don't treat me like an idiot."

"I'm not. I'm not. I'm not! Look, Mr. P, I didn't mean to. We're, err, so grateful to you, Mr. P. We both love you and think you're amazing."

Mr. Pyjamas lets go of Mrs. Sykes. She runs straight out of the bedroom, crying. She knows not to scream or alert anybody. It's not long before I can hear her being sick in one of the bathrooms. At least I know she's safe.

Mr. Pyjamas points his gun at my head as he tightens his grip.

"I'm doing all this work for you, kid, providing a better life with your wife. I can make it happen. Don't worry about how or why. That's all down to me. All you need to worry about is what you've got to do in return."

"That's, err, yeah, that's fair enough, mate."

"I'm not going to hurt you, kid. Or your wife. But I will do if you don't do exactly what I say. Got it?"

"Yes..."

Mr. Pyjamas slowly sits down on the bed. His leather trousers rip between the legs. I wonder if his balls will flop out and brush along the carpet. They are dangling back and forth, trying to hypnotise me. Mr. Pyjamas lowers his gun and slowly puts it back into his leather jacket pocket.

"Relax, kid. Then we can talk."

My face gets hot. It's scorching and burning. I imagine what I must look like to Mr. Pyjamas. A pig in clothes that's just been raped by its redneck farmers before been thrown into a pen for unbearably long and unnecessary torture. I look around the sizzling hot bedroom, feeling like I may be suffering from claustrophobia, everything goes blurry, feeling dizzy and losing my eyesight, getting increasingly agitated, shaking and shaking, clenching my fists.

I'm going to be sick. I'm going to pass out. I'm about to scream.

"Mr. Pyjamas!"

"Yep?"

"I'm ready to talk."

"That's my boy."

"What do you need me to do?"

"I need bodies, kid."

"Bodies?"

"I want both of your family's bodies. They're my family now."

"What do, err, what?"

"I want the bodies of both your families. I'll come back in a couple of days, three days, give you a chance to get things going."

"I don't…"

"It's for you to decide how to get me their bodies, kid. But if I come over in three days and y'ain't got at least one body for me to take, y'know what will happen?"

"Hmm."

Mr. Pyjamas stomps across the room with the sound of his leather thighs slapping together. He looks down at me from high up and takes off his sunglasses. His red daggers are sharply piercing into my eyes. The flames of hell burn through his retinas like he's looking through me.

"Are we on the same page?"

"Hmm."

"I need to hear a 'yes' from you, kid. Without a 'yes,' I'll be forced to drag your woman back into the room and shove this pistol in her mouth."

"Yes! Yes, we're on the same page."

"I believe you. This is why I've always liked you, kid. I'll see you in three days."

CHAPTER 2

I t's twenty-four hours later.
Everything is set up perfectly.

Booze. Balloons. Banners. Buffet.

Most of that cheap and dirty party bollocks.

Mrs. Sykes is wearing a flowery yellow dress. She looks beautiful. I'm unsure why, as she will be upstairs for the event.
"Ready for this, darl?"
"No."
"Y'know this is for the baby, right?"
"I'm not ready, but I will do it."
"Just remember what we said."
"I will."
"We tell him that he's the first one here, and he's early, and I'd like to give him a drink of whisky to have a toast. I'll tell him you'll be back in one hour, and the other guests will arrive soon."

"Got it."

"If anything seems off, like he tries to come upstairs, blabbed to other people, he's suspicious of the plan and can tell something is wrong with the whole shindig, then we pull out code red."

"Code red?"

"Y'know, I'll go into another room, pretend to be on the phone, tell him that you've been in an accident, you're in the hospital and need me to come, you're in critical condition."

"What if he wants to drive or offers to come along?"

"That's why I'll get him nice and drunk first. He's an alchi and a druggy, so he'll likely come fucked up anyway."

"What if none of this works?"

"We tell him it's all a prank. You come downstairs, and we'll say we're filming him for an online competition. He's been punked!"

"This all sounds ridiculous, if I'm honest, Mr. Sykes. No normal person would fall for this idiocy."

"It's a good job he's not normal."

"Got it."

"I love you, darl."

"I love you too."

"I love you, baby bump."

"Wuvz ye, dada."

Mrs. Sykes goes upstairs, leaving me in the garden.

She's sitting in our bedroom and listening.

I'm alone and panicking.

My pulse is racing like crazy, at least three beats per second.

Knock! Knock!

He's here!

Mrs. Sykes' second cousin.

I go to the front door and let him in.

"Whey up, my man!"

A shortish Scottish guy with curly black hair, an untidy black beard, bright blue eyes, and a grin like a Cheshire Cat bounces into the gaff. He's wearing patterned shorts, a multi-coloured Hawaiian shirt, and sandals. It looks like he's just got back from a beach holiday. His arms and legs are dangling everywhere, and he has a very thick accent. What is it with these bloody Celtics and their curly locks? He swaggers with self-confidence, limbs flying all over the place, acting like he's been offered one hundred blow jobs on his way here.

"Y'reet, Mr. Sykes?"

He rushes his way over to me and forcibly shakes my hand. He is screaming in my face with his thick Scottish accent and rubbing my hair with his sticky hands.

"Get off!"

I push his hands off my head. I can tell he's trying to embarrass me and put himself at the top of the hierarchy in my house. That isn't happening on my watch.

"Chill out, son. I'm just trying to say congrats!"

"I know, mate."

"Ah! Pure class. I'm so happy for yah both. Sorry I couldn't make it to the wake party, but I heard that it was a fucking belter, brah!"

He turns his back to me as though we hadn't just spoken and is bouncing his way into the garden with the energy of a rabbit. He starts to sing and seems like he's taken something. A line of coke, a bomb of MD, a gummy of speed. I follow him into the garden, stopping in the kitchen to pour him a massive whisky. The fact he's already taken drugs and off his head has done half of the work for me. I walk into the garden, and he's already acting like a fool. Maybe this won't be as hard as we first thought.

"I'm Ravemachine Dunter!"

"I know."

"No, no, no, yah don't seem to understand, my main man. I'm 'THE' Ravemachine Dunter."

"I know who you are, mate."

"Daah! Fuck off, yah wee Mary! There's no one alive who hasn't heard of 'THE' Ravemachine Dunter."

Interesting his use of the word 'alive.' Maybe he knows something? No, he's just a self-involved loser. Relax. He doesn't know anything. Let's calm down.

"I'm the one who invited you, Ravemachine."

Ravemachine gets right up in my face again. His nose nearly touching mine. Neither of us back down. Sweat drips from his forehead, and his breath reeks of beer. Standing opposite each other, he undoes a couple of his shirt buttons, purposely showing me his hairy chest.

"Whey! No problem, brah. Not a problem at all. I get yah trying to wind me up. That's fair enough, yah wee Mary. It's a big day for yah both. I can't wait to see Mrs. Sykes. When is everybody else getting here? Just know that everybody knows who 'THE' Ravemachine Dunter is!"

The cocky Scottish twat grins in my face and laughs his head off. Then, he goes back to chanting, ranting, and bouncing around the garden. He's absolutely off his rocker.

"Err, yeah, Mrs. Sykes is excited to see you. We were gutted that you couldn't reach my great aunt's wake. Mrs. Sykes should be back within the hour. Everybody else should get here pretty soon."

I think that I answered all of his drugged-up questions.

"Yah shitting me? I'm excited to see everybody, yah wee Mary."

"Please, can you stop calling me Mary?"

"Chill out, brah. Jesus. Sensitive Sally in the corner."

This idiot is unbearable. He's the cockiest, most self-obsessed, egotistical, annoying cunt I've ever met. I turn away from the bouncing rabbit and swig from the bottle of whisky in the corner. I'm praying this is all worth it. I'm putting everything and everyone on the line for this baby. In the corner, I mumble over my rehearsed lines and hear a big sniff from across the garden. I turn around and see Ravemachine sniffing white powder from a key. He runs around the garden, screaming. He grabs a chair, climbs up, nearly falls off, waves his massive bag of coke or speed into the air, and starts singing.

"Let's get this fucking started in here! Fucking started in here! Let's get this fucking started in here! Fucking started in here! Let's get this fucking started in here! Fucking started in here!"

"Shut up, Ravemachine."

I start to feel weird. The garden begins to go fuzzy, and my vision becomes blurry. I'm slurring my speech and forgetting what I'm saying. Ravemachine jumps down from the chair. He sniffs up for a couple of seconds, puts his keys and baggy away, wipes his nose with the back of his hand, and opens more buttons on his shirt so that it's half open and his semi-hairy chest is showing.

"Aye, wee man. Since yah asked me nicely. All yah had to do was be nice."

"Right, err, yeah. OK, I'm sorry. Can we, y'know, quietly do our own thing in separate corners, please? More people should be arriving soon."

"Aye, bro."

I take an intense breath as me and Ravemachine separate.

Ravemachine is on his digital pocket pad when I look over my shoulder. I can hear his voice coming out of the screen's speakers. It sounds like he's watching videos of himself online.

I keep reminding myself this is for the baby.

I'm excited. He's making me look forward to what I'm going to do. I didn't think I'd feel this way, but he's too much to handle.

Ravemachine is on his pad, laughing and cheering at videos of himself. At least he's left me alone. I hear Ravemachine pipe up from his position of parasitic cockiness, which takes on a life of its own and swallows those around him. Once you get swept up in the ego of somebody like Ravemachine, you'll never get out. He'll eat you for breakfast and drown you in a swamp of his ever-growing and vicious arrogance.

The baby, this is for the baby.

What if he's using his pad to contact other people? What if he's trying to find out where they are? When they're coming? If they're coming?

The baby, this is for the baby.

What if he's already spoken to them?

The baby, this is for the baby.
I can see that he's getting incredibly agitated. If I don't do it soon, he won't stick around. He'll contact others and realize this is a setup. The more fucked up he gets, the more suspicious he becomes. Everything is set up and ready to go inside the house. I need to get Ravemachine inside.

The baby, this is for the baby.

I'm going to do it.

The baby, this is for the baby.

I'm doing it now.

The baby, this is for the baby.

I walk over to him.

The baby, this is for the baby.

Pour another whisky.

The baby, this is for the baby.

He doesn't bat an eyelid!

The baby, this is for the baby.

What game is Ravemachine playing? Maybe he already knows? Maybe he's got his plan to wear me down with his drug-induced, self-obsessed, annoying Scottish personality?

I need to get him into the house asap.

I start to ramble to him about babies. Something that will irritate him as much as he's annoyed me. I begin my droning about babies right into Ravemachine's ear.

I'm droning on and on and on and on.

I don't bother leaving him. I don't intend to leave it. I've made a little nest beside him, a comfortable seat of security and status. I'm here for one reason and one reason only.

"I'm going to get myself a drink. Is that ahreet, brah?"

"Yeah, mate, plenty in the kitchen."

It fucking worked!

Ravemachine leaps up and makes his way into the house.

I see Ravemachine walk into the kitchen and the front room. I can hear him singing, 'Fuck the Queen! Fuck the Queen! Fuck the Queen! Fuck the Queen!'

I make my way into the kitchen. Everything is silent. Not a sound throughout the house. Something's wrong. I attempt to lightly jog back into the front room but trip over a loose floorboard. I don't go to the floor but nearly stand on a nail sticking out. I tidy myself up. I hear a sound coming from the front room towards the kitchen.

I turn towards the open food spread and cans of beer that cover the kitchen counter. I hear loud footsteps getting nearer and nearer.

"Is that you, Ravemachine?"

No answer.

The footsteps get closer and closer.

My heart is beating faster than it ever has in my entire life.

Ravemachine doesn't bother coming into the kitchen. Instead, it sounds like he's returned to the front room, making himself comfortable. Why is he quiet all of a sudden? I scurry from the kitchen into the front room. Ravemachine is standing by the window, smoking a cigarette.

"My good man."

"Yep, brah."

"Why were you stomping about outside of the kitchen?"

"I wasn't."

"Literally a couple of minutes ago."

"What are yah talking about?"

"You were about to come into the kitchen."

"I've not left this room since I came inside."

Ravemachine knows something isn't right. Everything falls silent. I glare at him. He stands in silence. He leans back near my great aunt's black leather sofa, moving from one leg to another. He stares out the window and sees all the cameras and security gates set up. CCTV and high fences.

I can hear Mrs. Sykes having an emotional breakdown upstairs. She's crying her eyes out and retching up her emotions, harsh sounds of spewing and crying. The ceiling and upstairs flooring are shaking.

I notice that Ravemachine's head is traveling in a specific direction. At first, I thought he was looking around the room. My eyes travel along the floor. I notice something. I follow Ravemachine's head movements and see what he's looking at. He's looking at the shining silver saviour. Mr Pyjamas instructed me to use this on our first test subject. This unique, selected pistol also comes with the famous golden bullet. Mr Pyjamas assured me that if I fired this golden bullet and hit him in the right place, I wouldn't need to worry about anything going forward. The golden bullet will take care of everything. It's already loaded into the pistol. I see its magnificence glow as the sunlight blazes through the double-glazed windows. I can genuinely hear soft, classical music playing in my head as the foretold brilliance of the pistol makes its way across the room. It's a selected pistol, just for me. But I'm an idiot. I accidentally forgot the pistol and left it in the corner, on one of the shitty worn-out chairs. Mr. Pyjamas will slap me if he finds out. Nobody should ever hold or look at the precious, shining silver saviour. Only he who is to use it.

Ravemachine notices that I've seen him keep looking at the pistol. We both know it's there. Nobody could avoid its spine-tingling powers, even if they wanted to. Its hypnotic energy could possess the very best of us and manipulate anybody into using it. I can see that Ravemachine has worked out the plan. This druggy knows our goal. It's not all my fault. Mrs. Sykes screamed the house down. So much for playing her part in all of this. It's down to me. Ravemachine quickly bounces from side to side, back and forth, foot to foot. He looks like he will make a move for the pistol. I dive for the chair! I beat him to it, grab the pistol and point it in his face.

He knows that I've got the better of him.

The pistol is a lot heavier than I imagined. It weighs my arm towards the floor. I quickly pull my arm up, straighten it and aim for his head. Then, I firmly click the trigger.

WOOSH!

The golden bullet springs out of the pistol. It's the quickest thing I've ever seen, traveling at the speed of light.

BANG!

Perfect shot.

Right in between his eyes.

His head splatters into pieces.

His face is completely unrecognisable.

Blood all over the walls.

No eyes. No mouth. No skin. Half a skull. Half a face. Half a brain.

I look around the room and see pieces of his flesh hanging from precious ornaments, swinging from the new chandeliers.

Holding the pistol to my chest, I frantically scrub the blood with my T-shirt. I am trying my best to avoid ruining this magnificent, handcrafted work of art. I hold the shining silver saviour in both hands, as its beautiful radiance almost makes me weep.

CHAPTER 3

I won't lie and pretend it wasn't worth it. I'm very grateful to have been allowed to show my loyalty to my family. Not many commoners are given such an opportunity. They use pointless words and lazy gestures. Some presents at Christmas and cards on your birthday. A couple of notes here and there to avoid actual responsibility. Genuine loyalty and commitment are values that real men will lay down their lives for.

It's only been a few days, but I've seen the way forward. I'm happy to carry the torch for my wife and child. I've shown Mrs. Sykes, bent my knee toward God, and, more importantly, proven myself to Mr. Pyjamas. Beyond that, I've proven to myself, and that silly little voice that lives inside my head, that I'm more than just a man. Whether she's ready to admit it or not, this is all very reassuring to Mrs. Sykes. She knows I can do anything to protect her and the baby. One of my main driving forces in life has always been to avoid turning out like any of the degenerates in my family. Whatever direction they've taken, I'll take the opposite.

Ravemachine didn't believe in violence. He was a drug addict, vegan, and radical activist who mouthed off endlessly about the environment, peace, and love. Where was the peace and love when he had half a gram of sniff blocking his left nostril? Mr. Pyjamas still won't tell us what he did with Ravemachine's dead body. That's for him to know and for us never to find out. Don't get me wrong, I felt guilty at first, but then I saw the magnificent outcome. Mrs. Sykes is still an emotional wreck and will be for some time. She is preggers, after all, and naturally in a highly emotional state. Mrs. Sykes' guilt will soon subside once she's had the baby and can see that what we did was all worth it. I calmed down within twenty-four hours when Mr. Pyjamas came to collect Ravemachine and gave me a good talking too. It actually worked! I woke up this morning feeling proud of myself. It's building my character and training me to be a great dad. I've decided that I'm going to stick to the signed agreement I made with Mr. Pyjamas.

Our new house has got even more significant, massive. Now we have six bedrooms, four bathrooms, a new fridge with an ice maker, triple-glazed windows, new taps, big TV with surround sound speakers, and a partridge in a pear tree. Neither of us had to lift a finger. It all came from the miracles of Mr. Pyjamas. That's not true. Blowing a Celtics head to pieces is raising more than a finger.

Waking up to bags and bags of money, we've got more cash than we know what to do with. It's spread all over the house. Underneath the bed, beneath the floor boards, shoved down the back of our multiple wardrobes.

Fifties, twenties, tens, Fifties, twenties, tens, Fifties, twenties, tens, Fifties, twenties, tens, Fifties, twenties, tens, Fifties, twenties, tens, Fifties, twenties, tens, Fifties, twenties, tens, Fifties, twenties, tens, Fifties, twenties, tens, Fifties, twenties, tens, Fifties.

Mrs. Sykes has woken up looking more beautiful than ever. No more disgusting stretch marks on her pregnant belly, the old lady's forehead wrinkles have disappeared, and her small boobs are round and incredibly perky. To top it all off, the most critical payment of all, the baby is fit, healthy, kicking, and on its way.

Not to mention how toned and ripped my body is. I've gone from a flabby mess to abs so solid that they would make a bodybuilder shit themselves. You could bounce walnuts off my abdomen and watch them spring to the ceiling. My bald patch has cleared up, and my hair is the thickest and blackest it's been in years since my early twenties.

Mrs. Sykes slowly flumps downstairs into the front room. I'm lying on the new, black leather sofa, sinking into its softness, coffee in hand with this massive mug from our new state-of-the-art, digitally robotic coffee maker.

"Morning. Want a coffee?"

"I'm alright, thanks."

"Come on. You've got to try it. It's incredible. The coffee maker is superior to what everybody else is drinking, and the beans are superb artwork. You've got to try it, Mrs. Sykes."

I can't help but call everything art. Everything is art. That's exactly how it feels, like we've been picked up and dropped into a painting by Monet or Manet.

"I don't want one, Mr. Sykes."

"Bad dream, again?"

"Yep."

"What about this time?"

"I don't want to talk about it."

"It's good for the baby to get things off your mind."

"I'm sure the baby will be fine."

"Honestly, you don't want the baby taking in any of your negative emotions."

"I'm not talking about my dream. I don't feel well."

"Right, OK. Fine. I'll tell you about my dream. I've had two strong coffees from that incredible machine. If I were ever to have sex with a robot, it would be with that coffee maker. That doesn't count as cheating, does it? Shagging a coffee maker. I don't think it does. Where was I? Err, oh, yeah! You've just woken up. I get it. You sit down here. This lovely, warm, new state-of-the-art leather sofa, I promise, will cheer you up. It is the most comfortable sofa I've ever sat on."

I jump to my feet and let moody Mrs. Sykes sit in my place.

"Put your feet up, darl. You've got to put your feet up to get the full leather sofa experience."

"I'm not arsed. I don't care about new coffee beans or machines. Look at the state of you after two coffees. I honestly don't give two shits about this sofa. It feels exactly like the old one. I especially don't care how ripped your abs are. They look quite girly. I preferred your old dad bod. You looked like a real man. I don't care about my big, fat round tits. They're annoying and hurt my back. I don't even care about the money. All I care about is our baby."

"Are you saying that I don't care about our baby? Because this has all been for our bastard baby. Everything I've said and done has been for our baby."

"I'm not saying that. It's just..."

"What?"

"Sometimes you sound so cold. The past couple of days, ever since, well, y'know…"

"Would you treat a suit-wearing city boy like this? If he was locked into a contract to scam millions on the stock market, would you fuck…"

"Listen to yourself. You sound ridiculous. I don't even know what you mean by that. You're so blasé about everything."

"I'm not blasé. I'm so grateful. This is all for the baby. It won't want for anything. Neither of us will."

I get down on my knees and hold Mrs. Sykes' hands.

"I'm happy because I have you and the baby. All of this means nothing without the two of you. So my happiness isn't coming from all the new stuff we keep waking up to. It's coming from enjoying it with the two people I love the most."

A huge smile comes across Mrs. Sykes' face. Ear to ear. The biggest grin that I've seen from her in a long time. She grabs my face and gives me a sloppy kiss on the lips, before pushing my head into her deep cleavage and making me motorboat those beach balloon knockers, for what feels like hours but is more like seconds. Finally, Mrs. Sykes lets me up for air. I stand up and trip backwards. I need a couple of seconds to catch my breath. Then, she starts laughing her head off.

The front room is chillingly quiet. Absolute silence. Neither of us says a word. Things are so quiet that all I can hear is the sound of the CCTV cameras attached to the roof moving from side to side. Finally, Mrs. Sykes pushes herself off the sofa. She slaps my hand out of the way as I try to help her up. She walks past me and doesn't make a sound.

Mrs. Sykes waddles back into the front room. Once again, I stand to give her my seat. Because I'm such a gentleman, I take one of the old, shitty, white kitchen chairs and plop it next to her. I want to show that I'm not just interested in our new stuff. Even if it does damage my back and make my ass cheeks go numb. I've already got a messed-up spine. Mrs. Sykes puts her feet up and sits on the lovely, comfortable leather sofa while I lean beside her. We both take a few deep breaths and try to relax. Nothing. Not a word.

Me and Mrs. Sykes both look in opposite directions. The room still reeks of her sick. It's livin' la reeker-loca! It's even worse upstairs. I've cracked open all of the bathroom and bedroom windows to breathe. That's one thing that hasn't calmed down, her levels of vomiting and shitting. I'm starting to get a bit worried. Before, we blamed her medication, and now we blame the baby. What if it's neither? There are so many questions that we can't answer.

Things will get even more complicated as we move forward. When our families start asking questions, the tax man wants us to show where we got our money, hospitals wonder why we aren't on the systems, and the list goes on and on. Neither of us has any answers to the difficult questions which await us.

Mrs. Sykes claims to be a very religious and moral woman. She believes in God. Not God as in, y'know, consciousness and space, but she thinks there's a man on a cloud, looking down on us. Some giant, old, grey-white cunt who only wears black. It sounds more like how the Devil should look, in my opinion.

Mrs. Sykes lethargically lies on her side and clutches her belly with both hands.

"Just think about how long we've been waiting for this."

Mrs. Sykes used to love moaning about her obsession with forehead lines. She thought she had wrinkles too. She didn't. Now she definitely doesn't. But Mrs. Sykes never listened. She had those tiny ears tightly stapled whenever I tried to tell her about wrinkles. She always used to say that if we came into a load of money, she would spend most of it on Botox and all of that other cosmetic shit. She's always been neurotic and overly emotional. She sobbed her heart out during my great-aunt's funeral. It wasn't her dead relative, but mine. If I wasn't crying, I don't see why she had to. People die, so what. A ninety-year-old wealthy lady has been taken from us. I didn't see anybody else helping her during the final days, just me. Nobody else in our families took her to the hospital and cared for her when she was on her last legs.

Mrs. Sykes seems as though she isn't willing to speak to me.

"I love you, Mrs. Sykes."

"I love you too, Mr. Sykes."

"I love you too, baby bump."

"Wuvz, you too, Daddy."

"Seeing you cuddled on the sofa like this is so cute."

"Thanks."

Mrs. Sykes pushes one of our brand-new cream pillows to her ear. I quickly stand up and briskly walk towards the door.

"I'll sort everything out. You lie there. Lie there and enjoy all of the luxuries that we get for free. Ungrateful bitch."

"What?"

I slap my hand over my mouth and rush out of the room before I say anything that could start World War Three.

CHAPTER 4

I'm inside the house, watching the rancid garden pool of mentally ill, germ-infested vermin. They can wait in the corners of the garden, watch the gloomy grey clouds, it's big enough, and I'll stay in my warm, heated kitchen. I'm talking, of course, about our family units. The blood-sucking parasites. No personality. No original thoughts. No thoughts at all. Whatever you want them to say or do, they will. They move and dance around like wooden marionettes. If they were all told they had to build a nuclear bomb and set it off in their basements, they would one hundred percent do it. Not a single member of our families could piece together the difference between the present and future consequences of their actions.

I'm not here to rant, and I'm not here to rave. I'm ready for my big moment. We've planned this to a tee. Mrs. Sykes is sitting upstairs and listening to me work my magic. Mr. Pyjamas told me I was his leading man and was there to do the job. He said I don't need to pretend to care about these assholes. They are our competition. People like this always will be. I go over the lines which me and Mrs. Sykes have rehearsed. I practice my actions as I'm waiting. I lean against the white kitchen wall, occasionally leaning over the sink, and flick through our plan.

The shining silver saviour isn't just any old pistol. It turns out that it reloads itself with one golden bullet after every successful shot. The shining silver saviour reproduces a hypnotic bullet, after a hypnotic bullet, after hypnotic bullet, after hypnotic bullet. But there's a catch. The first shot has to be successful. Mr. Pyjamas has pressed me to always aim for the head. It worked on Ravemachine, so I'll take that route as we advance.

I sneakily peek out the window and watch the few guests entertain themselves. They're all waiting for me to go outside. Like our first outing with Ravemachine, we've chosen family members we haven't seen in a while. Sworn them to secrecy and invited them over for a celebration. Using all the same rhetoric about how it's a surprise bash for Mrs. Sykes, people will be arriving soon, blah, blah, blah. Mr. Pyjamas wants his body count upped in numbers.

Mrs. Sykes' step-cousin and husband are here. Unlike the rest of our family units, these are well off and live a comfortable life. I'd say they're more upper-working class, maybe even lower-middle class. There was nobody else that we could think to invite who wouldn't ask too many questions. These two are polite and neurotic enough not to say anything. They aren't a part of the immediate family. Slight problem, though. They've brought their thirteen-year-old son with them! I don't know what the hell we're meant to do. Mr. Pyjamas wants results. He's waiting on action and has even threatened to take everything away from us. We thought this distant step-cousin and husband would be a great start. But now, a thirteen-year-old is here. I've been trying to get hold of Mr. Pyjamas all morning, but nothing. I think he's not answering on purpose.

"Hello, Mr. Sykes."

"Shit! I'm so sorry. You made me jump."

Mrs. Sykes' step-cousin drunkenly barges into the kitchen. We've given them whisky, peanuts, and wine. Wow! Up close, she looks like a sand viper. She's got hair the colour of golden sand. Amazing. Wait until I tell Mrs. Sykes that her step-cousin turned into a sophisticated sand viper, evolved from the garden, and into our kitchen. She has a very light Australian accent. She has piercing brown eyes that could hypnotize a Buffalo. This sand viper doesn't blink or smile. Instead, this Aussie flicks her sharp tongue at me and lets me know who's in charge with her long, bony witch's fingers.

"Are you OK?"

"Err, yes, I am, thanks, I'm, err, I'm good, thanks."

"I was just saying, I didn't know Mrs. Sykes was pregnant. How long have you been keeping it a secret?"

"Not too long."

"Interesting."

"It was, err, Mrs. Sykes' idea. Not mine. Y'know, with the funeral."

"I understand."

"Yep."

"How far gone is she?"

"I'm not, err, well, I'm not quite sure…"

"You're not sure how long she's been pregnant…?"

"Hmm."

"Oh, right."

"Hmm."

"You said Mrs. Sykes will be back soon?"

"Yep."

"How soon?"

"Half an hour."

"That's quite a while."

"Probably more like ten minutes."

"You said that the rest of the family would be here too?"

"Err, well, yeah, you're the first here. Nice and early."

"Oh, right."

"Hmm."

"Anyway, I won't keep you."

"Yeah, I'll, err, I'll be in the garden soon. I'm just preparing everything for the other guests. They shouldn't be too long."

My mind wanders away from reality. I'm incredibly drunk. Maybe she is a sand viper? I'm tripping from wall to wall, and I feel like I'm swaying side to side. I'm hyper-awake. I watch Sand Viper quickly slither around the garden. She's as thin as a skeleton and looks like she will eat me for breakfast. My eyes follow her around the greenery. Finally, we make it to the end of the road, and she turns toward her husband.

I'm sure this gathering is going to be a huge success. I'll show everybody back from the estate. Those who laughed, mocked, bullied, abandoned, and never believed in me. When they see what I've achieved they'll be the ones who feel stupid. Those who harassed and poked fun at me must deal with how wrong they were once they see how rich, successful, and attractive I eventually became. My family and friends will apologize, cry at my feet and beg for forgiveness. 'We're very sorry. What can we do to make you forgive us?'

I stare into the garden at their thirteen-year-old son. He speaks in a very posh accent and is dressed in all black, wearing an oversized dirty trench coat, black leggings, and thick boots. He won't talk to me. He sits in his own corner and whips off his big trench coat, swaggering like he's in a punk band. Hair up in a bun. He dresses poorly so that people think he's had a hard life. He's wearing a very tight 'Save the Environment' T-shirt as though the environment was a person who he could adopt. He could take the environment into his home, like a homeless tramp who needs a good scrub. He could put the environment into a nice comfortable bed, dress it in PJs' and read it a bedtime story.

I can see the son's hard nipples poking through the soft cloth. He glances at me through the window with utter scorn and disgust. I've never met somebody who I could tell hated me within a couple of seconds. He has a cute and naturally handsome face. But, on the other hand, he is barely even a teenager and is already smoking a vape pen. He will probably get a degree in Drama or English Lit. Deconstruct everything and everyone, from Dante through to Houellebecq. Something of the sort. He's way taller than me. Likely five-foot-eleven. Already! Very thin, never eats, milky skin, a great jawline, and a pointy nose.

I face away from the kitchen window and quickly twitch over my shoulder to see if Sand Viper is coming. I close my eyes and listen to the voices of the outside garden vermin. I want to know if they're talking about me. I hear the bony Sand Viper in her cold, light Australian accent. She mutters about the weather and if it's going to rain. No emotion or kindness whatsoever. She is the Sand Viper. Her greasy, golden hair dripped in wannabee-suffering and self-entitlement. We're taking the riches and spreading them to those who deserve it. This all belongs to me and Mrs. Sykes for our baby. I'm like Robin Hood! Take from the rich and give to the newborns.

I don't bother leaving my kitchen corner. I don't intend to leave it. I've made a little nest for myself. A comfortable den of security and status. Nobody has entered the kitchen. It's still just me. This is where I'm meant to be. So, I'm not nervous about doing this. Not at all. I said that I would take care of it. They need to get drunker. Then I'll bring them inside.

I hear the Catholic Daddy pipe up about me. He's very skinny, with hideously dry skin, thinning grey hair on top, cheeky child-like smile. He's very innocent, vulnerable, and sounds stupid. Anybody could take advantage and exploit him. I'm sure that's precisely what Sand Viper and The Son do. They dominate Catholic Daddy into doing whatever they want.

"He doesn't want to leave his corner, kiddo."

Catholic Daddy sounds like he's travelled forward in time from the old-time fishing docks.

"He's just waiting for everybody else to arrive. Well, that's the excuse he's going with. We should leave if nobody else has turned up by half past. I went inside to check on him, and he seemed very strange."

Fuck you, Sand Viper! You aren't going anywhere. Sand Viper and Catholic Daddy are getting suspicious of me.

My nose is pressed up against the corner of the kitchen wall. I want to focus on what they're saying about me. I'm waiting for the perfect moment to grab the shining silver saviour and do what needs to be done. The plan is to aim for a perfect shot between the eyes of our first guest. I guess that it's going to have to be Sand Viper. She's the strongest and most dominant. Hopefully, the golden bullet will reload, and I can hit Catholic Daddy straight in his forehead. As much as I don't want to kill The Son, I've no choice. I've got to protect my newborn child. I'm not doing this for me. This is for my wife and baby.

I hear the thirteen-year-old start to blab. The screeching and scrawling as he runs through his list of radical buzzwords. I can feel his man-hating eyes digging into my back, twisting my skin, breaking my spine, stomping and crushing my head with his enormous boots, ending it with pissing his dark green urine onto my bloodied face, all the while filming the event and circulating it on the internet. The video would get him praise and acclaim from my online haters. He will inspire activists throughout the country to come to hunt me down. They will turn up at the house, tear down the high gates, destroy the state-of-the-art security systems, boot down the door, and violently drag me, kicking and crying, down flights of stairs. They will lob me into the street, tear off my clothes, strip me naked, and slash and stab all my body with their blades and sharp knives. His activists will spray paint my body, rant, and rave about what an abusive bloke I am.

All will be competing to see who can win the online prize of the year! Thirteen-year-old wins yet again. He shoves my face into a paddling pool of blood, wraps several used tampons around my neck, and suffocates me until I pass out. The Son dives into the paddling pool, holds my head under, and drowns me with everybody else cheering and filming.

Mrs. Sykes will be a widow who has to raise our baby as a single parent. She won't be able to afford anything without me, and everything will be taken from her. Mrs. Sykes and the baby will spend days on the streets and will have to move back to a council estate. The actual council estate which we both escaped from and swore we'd never return.

Do I want Mrs. Sykes and our baby living in a council flat? Not a chance! Am I willing to do anything and everything to stop that happening? You bet I am! I'm not doing this for me. This is for my wife and baby.

Sand Viper and The Son bond over how late they were to the party. He has an incredibly posh accent combined with a massive cloud of strawberry vape, mixing his private education with his desire to be a member of a hard-done punk band. Sand Viper lists the many ways their travel here was delayed, making them incredibly late. Doesn't sound like too much of a hardship to me. The Son moves closer to the house. Sand Viper begins to get restless. She starts opening bottles of wine and pouring glasses of whisky. Catholic Daddy yawls and yelps in agreement. They get pissed as they wait for the other guests.

I slowly look over my left shoulder and see The Son take some money out of his coat pocket. He shoves it down his environmentalist T-shirt and pushes it into his chest. I move closer to the window. He accidentally drops some notes onto the glowing grass while shoving a load down his top. He knows that I'm watching her. Fuck. I wonder what I should do.

He bends down to pick up the notes and shows me his lacy, black thongs. The Son jiggles his ass at me and looks through his legs to see if I'm still watching. His black thongs are on full display for me to see. The Son slowly pushes himself up from the grass and rips down his radical T-shirt, showing me more of his chest. Sand Viper and Catholic Daddy are too drunk in the corner to see what's happening. The whole show was for my benefit. I quickly snap my head back around.

"Mr. Sykes is perving on me!"

The Son bellows at the top of his voice for all to hear. The kitchen walls vibrate like the strings of a guitar. He screeches and flicks her finger at me in accusation. I storm outside into the garden and defend myself.

"I've not done anything wrong."

I walk over to them and hold my hands up in defence.

"He gave me the creeps the moment I walked into the garden. I knew there was a reason that he stayed in the kitchen. To perv on all of us!"

"Take a look at yourselves, you bunch of nutcases. I've just been standing in my kitchen, quietly minding my business, quiet like a mouse."

"He tried to see my… he was going to touch my…"

The Son bursts into floods of tears.

"Come here, it's alright. He can't hurt you now."

Sand Viper takes him in her arms. She consoles The Son, who sobs into Sand Vipers' flabby chest. I look at them both. The Son stays on Sand Viper's shoulder. Sand Viper gives me evils. She makes the slitting motion with her finger, trying to suggest that she wants to cut my throat.

"You're insane. I've just been standing in the kitchen and minding my business."

"He's smiling, the disgusting perv."

"I'm smiling at how ridiculous you're all been."

"I say we all grab the little pervert. What do you think, Daddy?"

The Son tries to round up the mob.

"I'm not getting involved, kiddo."

"What do you think, mum?"

The Son asks for Sand Vipers' advice. He pulls her overly emotional face away from mummy's chest before screaming at me! All the while still having his perky nipples on full display for the whole garden to see.

"I say we tie him up and roll him into the middle of the garden."

"Please, can we all just calm down? This is meant to be a family celebration."

I try to reason with them, but the mob turns against me as they bare their torches.

"Let's get him!"

Sand Viper and The Son move toward me. They both look like they're ready for some hideous emotional violence. I have no choice. I'm going to have to take them all out. This is the perfect time. I sprint into the front room, grab my silver pistol and run outside. I've got one golden bullet that I need to hit perfectly.

I'm not doing this for me. This is for my wife and baby.

Sand Viper is holding a broken bottle of wine. She attempts to come at me but drunkenly stumbles from side to side, eventually falling onto the grass. Legs up in the air, showing her old-lady granny panties. The booze has hit Sand Viper so hard that she rolls around and looks like she's forgotten what's happening. Catholic Daddy is just sitting in the garden corner, not getting involved, like the pathetic worm that he is.

Just as I take my eyes off Sand Viper and Catholic Daddy, I see crazy, posh The Son run across the garden, screaming and yelping with a kitchen knife in his right hand. He steps towards me and aims for the side of my neck with the blade, slash, slash, slash. He misses my neck. I manage to step to one side, but the heavy pistol weighs down my arm. I drop it to the ground, and he aims the blade at my head, stab, stab, stab. I jump to one side. He sees the pistol and screams at me! I manage to boot him straight in the right knee. He quickly collapses to the ground, drops the knife onto the grass, clutches his right knee in agony, straightens his left leg, and rolls onto his back in pain.

Sand Viper comes out of nowhere. She tries to stab me with the broken bottle, but the whole thing shatters in her hands. Shards of wine bottle pierce her skin.

There's blood everywhere as the two women clutch themselves in agony and roll on the ground.

At last, the scared and pathetic Catholic Daddy stands up. He begins swearing at me, which is not a very religious or Godly thing to do. I finally snatch the shining silver saviour from the grass and shoot a golden bullet.

WOOSH!

The golden bullet fires at the speed of light.

He turns away from me.

BANG!

That is another perfect shot.

This time in the back of his head.

His head explodes across the garden into a hundred little pieces.

Sand Viper loses so much blood from her hand that she passes out.

The Son screams and stumbles into the house.

I follow him inside and try to fire the pistol.

It's still not reloaded.

He hobbles his way to the front door. I sprint into the house. He trips over the loose floorboard, steps on the nail that lodges into his foot, trips over the kitchen step, and smacks his head on the solid side. I slam the backdoor shut. The Son tries to push himself up from the kitchen floor but repeatedly falls back down.

I stomp on his hand.

"Argh!"

My boots trap his fingers.

"Argh!"

I stomp on his hand repeatedly, as hard as I possibly can.

"Argh!"

I'm trying to break all of his fingers.

"Argh!"

I stand over The Son, aim the shining silver saviour at his head, and fire.

The pistol doesn't fire. I check, and it hasn't reloaded. I thought the magic golden bullet reloaded. What the hell is going on? Why won't this thing work?

I look out the kitchen window, and Sand Viper crawls to Catholic Daddy. She screams and cries. My eardrums have burst from all of the ridiculously loud whining. Why won't they die quickly and quietly?

I look down at a whimpering The Son. If the golden bullet doesn't reload, I have no other choice. I'm going to have to do this the old-fashioned way. I slowly lift my boot from his crippled hand. His fingers are bent in ways I didn't know were possible. I scramble around the kitchen, looking for something to choke him with. All the while reminding myself I'm not doing this for me. This is for my wife and baby. Which reminds me, I've not heard a single peep from Mrs. Sykes all evening. She must have finally come around to the idea this is what's best for all of us.

We've got cable rope underneath the sink! I grab the cable rope and twist it around my hands.

"I promise this won't take long."

I'm not doing this for me. This is for my wife and baby.

CHAPTER 5

I never thought I'd be sitting on such an expensive toilet.

One of many around our house. A diamond seat with a first-class cleaning system. The bog essentially cleans your asshole without you having to lift a finger. Or hand. You don't even have to move your legs or feet. There's no need for that old school, poor people, toilet roll idiocy. Only gammons smear poo particles into their hairy cracks. Don't get me wrong, that was the life that we used to live. Even worse. Sometimes we'd run out of toilet roll and have to use our hands. I've known many, many, many people who have done so. But not anymore. No, no, no! This is a rich man's product. It has immaculately designed taps attached to the inside of the bog, spraying fresh, clean water directly into your bum. Then a thin brush with some sponge attached to the end that feels like a feather duster comes out of the bottom and starts scrubbing your bum hole. I doubt we'll buy toilet roll if this is the life we're destined to live. The way things are going, it seems to be.

This isn't a big deal in Japan. They're the height of technological sophistication and impeccable manners. But they're also at the height of low birth rates, suicide, and abuse of the elderly. So, I doubt having one of these toilets in every house will lead to anything revolutionary. But if you weed out the riff raff and just let the high-class Westerners have one, there will be much more appreciation and something for the lower mobility to work towards. So, keep those class divisions in place. Keep the scum of the estate away from my toilet.

I sit on the incredible, glowing diamond seat and watch Mrs. Sykes in the bubble bath. It's long and deep, with a button that sets off a bubble machine in the tub, like a jacuzzi. It buzzes against your genitals if you squeeze and squish them against the vibrating jets. Mrs. Sykes has lost all respect and appreciation for everything I've worked for. She's happy to use one of our state-of-the-art bathrooms, sleep in one of our substantial triple beds, lie on one of the comfortable leather sofas, watch mind-numbing 3D digital crap, wear brand-new designer clothes, cook delicious healthy food out of the self-refilling kitchen.

How did we get all of this?

God looks down on us and gives us whatever we want whenever needed.

But I've played my part too.

I planned, plotted, invited, arranged, set up, introduced, poured, laughed, panicked, loaded, shot, dragged, wrapped up, cut up, tied up, exchanged, shook hands…

Mrs. Sykes never comments on anything. She never says 'thank you' or how much she enjoys our material possessions and household appliances. She will never mention any of the jobs I've done to take us from estate scum to a luxury lifestyle. She would be shitting into a bucket and sleeping on the floor if it wasn't for me. Best of all, the thing I wish that Mrs. Sykes would be most grateful for, I've got us out of the public health service. We're having this baby through private health care. We won't have to pass a smackhead in the corridor as he picks up his methadone. We won't have to lie or sit next to some twenty-one-year-old who can't read and write but is somehow allowed to give birth to child number five. We won't have to listen to the screams of an old, dying pensioner who has fallen down the stairs for the eleventh time this week and still refuses to go into a care home. We'll get the best treatment from paid and private health services. Like the English King, Saudi Prince, or Elvis!

I watch Mrs. Sykes lying in the bath with her eyes closed. Her head rested on a specially designed pillow, and her legs stretched out, still unable to reach the other side. Her humongous boobs plonked on top of her chest with massive nipples pointing towards the glittering ceiling chandeliers and preparing the healthiest, most fabulous breast milk for our baby. I press my feet onto the warm and heated floor, lean my ass cheeks into the cosy and fluffy toilet seat, and push my head forward to talk to Mrs. Sykes. I stop myself and go back to gawping at her.

I keep having this recurring daydream about Mrs. Sykes in our new bath. The dream quickly fills my imagination whenever I sit on this toilet seat and have my hole scraped. It's like I've just been given a spaceship to race up to another planet and save it from the witch's magic.

In the dream, I'm watching Mrs. Sykes wash. She begins farting in the bath. Very loud. Water waves splash up towards the ceiling, drenches the heated floor, and damages the water system. A gigantic love-heart-shaped fart bubble floats into the air. It makes its way toward me and quickly sucks me inside.

The love-heart bubble manages to hold my weight and doesn't seem like it will ever pop. I scream for Mrs. Sykes' help as the love-heart bubble stops oxygen from getting inside. I'm cut off from breathing as the love-heart bubble travels around the bathroom. I am twisting and twirling in circles, like an Operatic performance or a Gymnast training for the Olympics. Mrs. Sykes ignores me. She thinks I'm being dramatic and has no intention of engaging with me. I slowly die inside the love-heart bubble. I'm still forcibly trapped and tightly contained inside as it floats out of the bathroom door, through the big open window, over the colossal garden fence, past the security cameras, and throughout our privately green lands.

The love-heart bubble spends hours and hours floating throughout the lands, into the city, eventually taking me back to the dreaded council estate. The love-heart bubble finally pops. My dead body violently drops from the sky and splatters on the doorstep of our old accommodation. The little kids who now live there come outside to play. They're about ten or eleven. They scoop my watery remains up from the ground and pour me into a foam cup. One of the kids is dared to drink my remains. He does. A couple of hours later, he pisses me into his dirty, grimy, horrible toilet. My watered-down, piss body swims through the sewers. I travel around the city drains near mine and Mrs Sykes' multi-acre land. I get sucked into the pipes, feel myself sail out of some taps, and splash into a bathtub. My watery remains swim in the tub water. I look up and see Mrs. Sykes. I'm back where I belong in the bath with Mrs. Sykes.

"Every morning, I wake up with that war-time mentality."

"Ha! Did you just say war-time mentality?"

"Yeah, I did, Mrs. Sykes. Top button is done up. Pull yourself up by your bootstraps."

"You sound like an idiot."

"Piss off."

"It won't be long before you sing God save the Queen, jumping about on the table."

"One time that happened."

"Just let me relax and enjoy my bath."

I'm fed of this. She turns her nose up at anything I say and everything I do.

"Do you have nothing else to say?"

"How many more times are you going to ask?"

"Well, I'm just making sure, aren't I?"

"Is that what you're doing?"

"Fuck's sake, come on, don't be like that."

"Like what?"

"Moody. Ungrateful. Spoilt."

"I'm not any of those things."

"Criticising everything that comes out of my mouth."

"If what came out of your mouth wasn't utter shit, then we'd be fine, wouldn't we?"

I sink my head into my hands and lean forward.

"Wouldn't we?"

"I'm not answering that. But, again, you're trying to make me look like a dick head."

Mrs. Sykes, still with her eyes closed and nipples erect, exhales with frustration.

"You're so distant and sarcastic whenever you talk to me. Not everything has to be tarted up with sarcasm."

"I'll stop with the sarcasm when you stop blabbing about all this materialistic nonsense."

"Deal."

I sit and scowl at Mrs. Sykes as she lies there with her eyes closed.

Mrs. Sykes gets a pain in her stomach.

"Fuck!"

"What is it?"

Mrs. Sykes shoots up into a sitting position.

"My belly..."

"What's wrong?"

"I think the baby's coming."

"The…?"

"Yes!"

I run over to the bath and try to comfort Mrs. Sykes. I'm baffled. Mrs. Sykes puts her hands on her belly and starts becoming emotional. It all makes me extremely uncomfortable. Pregnancy, baby pains, all of that stuff. We've avoided this subject for some time, possibly with good reason. We both contemplate what to do next. Mrs. Sykes gets another sharp pain in her belly. She cringes in pain as she tries to control it. The pain gets worse, and she can't handle it.

Mrs. Sykes screams out in pain!

What do I say? What am I meant to do? I'm not good with babies. I've not got the training.

I eventually help Mrs Sykes out of the bath, and she goes down onto the floor. She is crawling about on her hands and knees. Mrs. Sykes makes noises that I've only seen in wildlife documentaries. Why couldn't God give us some golden medication for our birth? If God is so magical. Or maybe some golden earbuds for me?

"What's happening?"

I try to place his hands on Mrs. Sykes."

"No! Argh!"

"Can you move?"

"I don't know."

I try to help Mrs. Sykes from the floor, but it only worsens things.

She screams out in pain!

"Right, I don't know what to do. Tell me what to do."

I walk around the bathroom, scared and frustrated, still pissed off."

"Just leave me."

"We've got to get you to a hospital."

"How?"

"I'll drive us."

"Argh!"

She screams out in pain.

"You can't drive."

"I can. I don't have a license, but who cares about a badge with your photo on it."

I walk around the bathroom as Mrs. Sykes crawls about the floor. I think about my next move.

"We're going to get you up, take you to hospital, and I don't care if I get a fine or prison for driving without a licence and breaking their stupid rules. So you're going to be alright, yeah?"

"I hope so."

"I promise, darl."

"Argh!"

She screams out in pain.

"I promise that everything will be alright."

"Fine. Argh!"

She screams out in pain.

"Right, this might hurt a bit. Ready?"

I grab Mrs. Sykes from behind, underneath her arms, leaning her back against my abdomen. I go to lift her from the warm, toasty bathroom floor.

"One, two, three…"

I manage to lift Mrs. Sykes onto her feet slowly. Water has splashed onto the floor as our wet soapy feet slip and slide on the oily bathroom tiles.

She slips backwards.

"I've got you."

I catch her.

"Argh!"

She screams out in pain.

She slips backwards.

"I've got you."

I catch her.

"Argh!"

She screams out in pain.

She slips backwards.

"I've got you."

I catch her.

"Argh!"

She screams out in pain.

She slips backwards.

"I've got you."

I catch her.

"Argh!"

She screams out in pain.

She slips backwards.

"I've got you."

I catch her.

"Argh!"

She screams out in pain.

We both hobble to the bathroom door. Her arms wrapped around my shoulders. It's time to get ready and have this baby. The time has come for us to give birth.

It's one week later.

Mrs. Sykes has been in the hospital with me by her side, and we managed to get through everything. It's been a couple of days since the birth of Baby Owl. After nearly losing Baby Owl, she is now safe and sound. She will soon be home with everything she could ask for. Of course, Mrs. Sykes and Baby Owl will be spoilt rotten. But not just in some shallow, hollow, materialist way, but with the finest essentials that money can buy. Excellent education. Top-notch hobbies and interests. Private health care. Incredible family holidays.

I help Mrs. Sykes safely through our electronic gates, turn off the alarm systems, and slowly assist her into our house.

"Watch your step."

"Thank you."

We walk into the front room, and I get Mrs. Sykes into her seat.

"One, two, three…"

I slowly lower Mrs. Sykes onto the comfortable leather sofa.

"Mr. Sykes…"

"Yes?"

"I know you're just trying to help, but you've been helping me in and out of chairs for the past week. I think that I'm fine to sit down by myself."

"Yeah, sure, sorry."

"It's fine."

Mrs. Sykes stretches out across the sofa.

"Home sweet home."

"Yep."

"At least it got us out of the house for a bit."

"Yep."

"Sometimes you need an emergency to make you see sense."

"You're not wrong, Mr. Sykes."

"Keep your feet up. I'm going wait on you hand and foot."

"My own servant."

"At your service, madam."

"My little bitch boy."

"Ha! Good one…"

"At least everything's fine with us, though."

"I'm so glad that you're both alright."

"Me too."

"How do you feel?"

"Sore."

"I bet."

"And hungry."

"What can I get you?"

"What? "

"What can I get for you?"

"No, I heard what you said, just surprised."

"Why?"

"Offering to cook for me."

"I've offered to cook before."

"How did that go again?"

"I burnt all of it, we chucked it in the bin, and then we got a pizza."

"How did you manage to burn pasta?"

"Complicated."

"It isn't."

I sit next to Mrs. Sykes on the sofa. She puts her legs over me and lies back. We both smile and enjoy each other's company.

"I'm so grateful that you're alright."

"Me too."

Me and Mrs. Sykes have a quiet moment.

"I love you."

"I love you, too. Both of you."

Mrs. Sykes looks up and smiles at me. She gives me a soft kiss on both my cheeks.

"A blessing in disguise."

"I can't wait until she comes home."

"Me too."

"When can we go collect her from the hospital?"

"They said we could have her home within a few days."

"Amazing."

CHAPTER 6

I steadily walk out of the kitchen door and across the garden. I'm carrying a round metal tray to our wooden outdoor table. I watch my every step not to trip over and drop anything onto the neatly cut grass.

The last thing we need on such a big day is a physical injury. My stomach is already in knots as it is. This could be our final interaction with Mr. P. If everything goes well for us, theirs hope this could all be over. Whereas, if things don't go as planned, it's safe to say we could be dragged out of our comfort zone. I dread to think what will happen to us. My soul belongs to the Devil, so the fiery depths of hell could be right around the corner. Mr. Pyjamas has demanded the bodies of every remaining member of our families. He even went so far as to threaten Baby Owl's life! I shake angrily and tremble with fury at the thought of his threats. My pulse races and my blood pressure rises to that of an eighty-year-old having a heart attack. But I've trained myself in discipline and delayed gratification throughout this roller-coaster experience.

So, we've planned a big family barbecue. Mr. Pyjamas can have his way and take their bodies. We consider these people as ex-family members. Your family is the one that you make yourself. Not the womb you're forced to live in for nine months, like a massive dog crammed in a metal cage, or the hole you are dragged out of for several hours, bloodied and screaming your heart out. And, especially not the upbringing to which you have no control whatsoever. You're teetering on the brink of being a crack addict or molecular biologist. Depending on who, where, and how you're raised. A radical gamble and unfair feelings of thrownness.

I carefully lower the tray onto the wonky table. I remove the lid to reveal a buffet full of meats, cheeses, fruits, and wines. We've set up a beautiful spread in our back garden. However, my insistence on some new garden furniture has proven correct. The cold, continental meats, posh cheeses, and fresh fruit all glow in the back garden sun with colourful radiance. The dark redness of the pepperoni and salami looks so detailed that I feel like I've taken a tab of acid with exciting specs and dots, which I would never usually notice or be interested in. The green apples and yellow bananas shine like a rainbow in the sky. The red and white wines sparkle and pop, propping up the sophistication of our family gathering. We're now living in a celebratory victory that we can both be proud of. Tall oak trees and leafy bushes, the kind you see in a children's nursery rhyme book, old-school swings, and slides for kids to play on in the glorious outdoor world of wonder. Archetypical rows of traditionally built houses with stone bricks and a small fireplace that lights the room to look like an old log cabin.

Mrs. Sykes is a lot calmer than me. It's probably because she knows I'm the one who will have to carry out the big jobs and deal with the consequences if all goes wrong. She knows her loving husband will sacrifice himself to save his family. And she's entirely right! I dragged Mrs. Sykes into playing this game. She never really wanted any of it. Like everything in life, there is a cost and sacrifice that needs to be made to get anything you want.

I'll forever be drowning in the deep sea to which there's never any land to swim. Just when I think I've found a tiny island to clean myself up, one which will save my life and help me escape from hell on Earth, I'm dragged back under and left to drown in another cycle of life I can never escape. I was born and will die for this. Not by will or by intention but by force. Destiny controls my life events, circumambulations, epochs, and behaviour patterns.

The biggest life lesson I've learned is that decadence kills. It kills like nothing else I've ever seen. Decadence makes cancerous tumours and undiagnosed degenerative diseases look like luxury holidays to the Caribbean islands in comparison. The clear blue sky and the bright yellow sun give me a sense that God is at one with us again.

Just as I shovel thick slices of ham into my mouth and gulp down a bottle of white wine, Mrs. Sykes walks outside, clips me around the head, and gives me a dirty look.

"What?"

"Stop behaving like a pig."

"I'm not. I'm eating pigs."

I deny this fact while choking on a slice of ham.

"People will be arriving soon."

"Yep."

I stop scoffing the scran and instead focus on washing it down with white wine, using just one hand to gulp it straight from the bottle. The booze brings forth confidence while calming the anxiety.

"Is she asleep?"

"Hmm."

Mrs. Sykes makes me feel like a drunken idiot before she goes back inside. Ah, well. All seems fine with the food. I take one final look and then walk around the garden in a circle. With the bottle of white wine dangling beside me as I take huge gulps until the bottle is finally gone! I've drunk an entire bottle of wine to myself in just under half an hour. We're celebrating the birth of our daughter while waving goodbye to our tormentor. Who cares if I get a bit tipsy?

I peacefully skim my shoes against the neatly cut grass. It's incredible how something so simple can make me feel at ease. I crack open bottle number two and have a couple of swigs of red wine. Hmm! Hello Mr. Delicious. I breeze back into the kitchen, holding Mr. Delicious by my side as though we've recently got engaged and holding hands to express our genuine love for one another. Mrs. Sykes joins me.

"Baby Owl is fast asleep."

"Bless her."

"Are you still drinking?"

"Listen, I'm fine. We're celebrating! Aren't we? That's what we're telling our guests. This is one huge family celebration."

"Yeah, I know, but…"

"It's all fine when theirs wine. I'm just enjoying a little drink while I think about how grateful I am to have such a beautiful wife."

"Right…"

"Do you want to taste Mr. Delicious?"

"Mr.…?"

"Mr. Delicious. He's my bottle of red wine."

"Nice name."

"Thanks. We're in love."

"Ha, err, no, I'm good, thanks. Better keep a clear head for the family."

"Yeah, sure, no worries."

"Just try not to get too drunk. We don't want a repeat of last time. No fighting."

"That wasn't my fault."

"You were involved."

"Woodhead is an evil, sneaky, Machiavellian twat. Your sister can do much better than that lying piece of shit. He opened my eyes to how sneaky Mancs are. You've got to watch out for them, Mancs. If Jesus were alive today, his Judas would be a Manc. I guarantee it."

"Alright, alright. Calm down."

"You brought it up."

"Just play nice, yeah. This is Baby Owl's big day. We're celebrating her, not you."

"I know we are."

"Luckily for you, Woodhead isn't coming."

"Shame. I would have loved to have poisoned him."

"Follow my plan, and there will be nobody else to worry about."

"Good."

"Only if you follow my plan, Mr. Sykes."

"I will.

"Do we need to go through it, again?"

"Bloody hell, I'm not that drunk."

"The three of us need to stick together."

"Together forever, babe. Me, you, and Baby Owl."

"I love you, Mr. Sykes."

"I love you too, Mrs. Sykes. You've planned this to perfection. You're the genius."

I take a massive swig from Mr. Delicious. Downing half of the bottle and feeling like I will spew on the floor. I smash the back of my head against the fridge and tumble forward.

Neither of us says a word. Mrs. Sykes leaves the kitchen to check on Baby Owl. I stare outside at the beautiful, clear blue sky. I walk into the garden and sway from side to side. I finally reach the wonky table and shove handfuls of salami, pepperoni, pastrami, cheese, and bloomer bread into my gob. I choke like an obese man eating his seventh meal of the day. Five to ten minutes later, I stop, turn away from the table, and vomit all over the grass. I spew for at least a couple of minutes. It's light brown and dark yellow with huge chunks of food. I wipe the sick off my face and stumble across the garden.

I dragged Mrs. Sykes into playing this game with Mr. Pyjamas. She doesn't want any of it. Only Baby Owl and our happy life in nature. I enjoy all of the material nonsense and going through with the things we had to do to get it.

I emerge from the table, then stagger across the garden and into the house.

An hour or so later, I've moderately sobered up. I stand by the front door and anxiously wait for our first guest. I'm dressed very smartly, changing out of my clothes which I vomited on. I'd go as far as saying I'm looking snazzier than at the great aunt's funeral. I'm wearing a new, luxurious dark blue suit, black shoes, and a thick gold designer watch. My hair is gelled back to mimic the style of a camp fitness model, and my beard is shaped to mirror the look of a rugged movie star. I'm holding a whisky with ice and waiting for the first guest to arrive. After a while, I down my whisky and go into the kitchen to get another. I was nearly slipping on a wet and sparkling floor and gripping the wall to stop myself from ending up on my ass.

I breeze over to the table like James Bond. There's a huge glass bowl of homemade poisoned punch, which me and Mrs. Sykes have spent the past few hours making. Oceans of alcohol filled to the top. We've got vodka, gin, whisky, brandy, rum, and colourful alcopops to soften the extreme taste and add a splash of brightness to the event. Both of our family units are pissheads. We plan to sell the poisoned punch as a celebratory drink and a double dare. You're not tough enough to try it. Any chance to knock booze back will be enough for our lot to raise a toast. But if not, we've always got the blackmail aspect of them being weak little pussy. Something their low intelligence would gullibly lead them into.

Along with the eye-watering spirits and rainbow pops, we've managed to crush and ram bottles, bottles, and bottles of various tablets into the bowl of punch. We've mixed it in for hours so that nobody can taste it. There were hundreds of crushed-up tablets, Mrs. Sykes' anti-anxiety pills, co-codamol, sleeping tablets, and anything we had in the house.

This isn't a slow process. I've got to be incredibly efficient and quickly race this mission to its finish line. Listen, we don't want to do this! But we want to save the life of our gorgeous newborn Baby Owl.

As I add more tasty flavours to the poisoned punch, Mrs. Sykes stands on the grass in the scorching heat. She sets up the outdoor buffet with the orange sun blazing down on her. There are also a couple of deposable barbecues on the outdoor tables and packets of meat in our expensive, state-of-the-art kitchen fridge.

Burgers, steaks, sausages, ribs, bacon. The food and drink display will be so big that nobody within the family units will question what we're serving them. The hundreds of tablets will flow nicely with the extravagant spread that we've put on for them. Thankfully Baby Owl is asleep upstairs. Throughout the evening, we'll go up, one after the other, to repeatedly check on her. If anybody even thinks about going to see her, then I'm afraid they'll be taking a golden bullet. I like to think that me and Mrs. Sykes have all basis covered.

If Mr. Pyjamas isn't grateful for all of this and doesn't appreciate the effort we've obviously put in, my respect for the man will seriously decrease. Even if his chest and arms are getting bigger, I'll admit that I was a massive fan of the bloke when he provided us with tits and abs, beds and baths, clothes and phones, sofas and televisions, cars and cash, but now our baby daughter is involved. It's changed everything. Mr. Pyjamas is no longer a threat to just our material objects. Things are deep and personal, so we're willing to get today over with no matter what. If we have to see every single member of our families drop dead at our feet, or burn like candle wax under bricks, then so be it.

Crack!

Crack!

Boom!

Boom!

It's the front door. Right. Here we go. Play it cool, general. This will be easy-peasy and over in no time. I peek out the kitchen window and give Mrs. Sykes the thumbs up. Now is the time to act out the plan as we rehearsed it.

Crack!

Crack!

Boom!

Boom!

A couple of louder knocks. I sort out my expensive tie and confidently swagger out of the kitchen and down the hall. I unlock the bolts and chains and pull the door open.

I freeze.

Shit.

It's Mr. Pyjamas.

He's wrapped in black leather from head to toe. He is holding a motorcycle helmet under his arm. The blistering sun shines on his jet-black quiff and twinkles from his sunglasses. Mr. Pyjamas embodies a 1950s biker like Danny from Grease the musical.

"How're y'doing, kid?"

"I err, didn't, err, I didn't know you were coming."

"Neither did I. But it's a big job, so I thought I'd come to support you."

"That's, err, yeah, mate, that's nice of you."

"Thanks, kid. Now let me in and get me a drink."

Mr. Pyjamas rudely barges past me and knocks me to one side. I'm more well-dressed than he is. A sharp suit that makes me look like I'm going for a drink in an expensive city cocktail bar. You wouldn't think I chucked my guts up a few hours ago. I bounce back quickly, no matter the circumstances. At the same time, Mr. Pyjamas looks like he's drinking whisky in a Kentucky redneck shack. I follow Mr. Pyjamas inside and close the door.

"What's this, kid?"

He shouts at me from the kitchen. As I catch up with Mr. Pyjamas, I see him sniffing the poisoned punch. I quickly run over to him. Argh! Nearly slipping on the wet floor.

"Don't touch that, Mr. P! It's poisoned punch."

"What's that?"

Mr. Pyjamas whips out his comb and brushes his enormous quiff.

"It's an alcoholic punch we've poisoned with hundreds of tablets from various medications."

Mr. Pyjamas pushes the comb into his jacket pocket. He pulls out a cigarette, lights up, and starts smoking. Clouds and clouds of smoke fill the entire kitchen. We both stare at each other. The atmosphere is incredibly tense. He looks like he hates my plan, and I loathe his existence. Mr. Pyjamas doesn't respond. He walks into the garden. I notice him staring at Mrs. Sykes as the pair have an awkward conversation about how the weather is scorching for this time of year. As I go to help Mrs. Sykes, there's another knock at the front door. She gives me the nod to answer and says that she will handle Mr. Pyjamas. I unlock the chains and bolts and pull the door wide open.

It's Gran Sykes and Grandad Sykes!

Standing there with their round glasses and false teeth, both crouched over, gripping their walkers. Gran Sykes has thinning grey hair, which she consistently bleaches blonde every month. It makes the hair thinner, a clear fact that she repeatedly denies. She's so in denial about the effect dying her hair has that she blames the environmental decline for it falling out.

Gran Sykes has a round face with at least three or four moles spread across her chubby cheeks. She has a turkey neck and quite a chunky body while carrying all her weight in the lower part. Obese ass and thick hips. Apart from that, she's in excellent health. But you wouldn't think it from looking at her. Gran Sykes has a severe case of Munchausen syndrome. She loves the attention and power that looking sick gives her. The sympathy from strangers on the street, randomers on the internet, or even close friends and family, is enough to make her falsify and lie about having health issues. She even tries to make herself ill so that others will continue giving her the attention she desperately craves.

For starters, she's wearing a hearing aid in her left ear. I am still determining how she managed to get it fitted. She probably lied to the doctors and fibbed her way through the tests. She can hear better than me during events like the great aunt's funeral. She had her hearing aid turned off, yet throughout the afterparty could speak across the garden and pass on information like a fit and healthy teenager with spot-on hearing. Yet she would be the first to bring up how terrible her ears were, especially to strangers. It's usually her first topic of conversation with people she's just met. But I can always see the enormous grin across her face whenever anybody asks about the hearing aid. She gets the violins out and tells a pack of lies to obtain the reward of power.

Gran Sykes also shifts about with a walker. Again, this is the Munchausen syndrome kicking in. She doesn't need it and constantly posts videos of her using it online. Even the videos are evidence she doesn't need it. She unknowingly shows what a quick and swift walker she is while also trying to grab onto some sympathetic words of compassion. I've seen her multiple times, after she's had a drink, swipe it to one side and have a dance. As soon as she realises that she's been spotted she returns to the walker and rambles on about how weak her legs are.

On top of that, she's vulgar. Gran Sykes openly swears in front of everybody. She loudly farts and burps in public. She elbows people in their ribs and whines to get attention.

Before I can speak, Gran Sykes rudely pushes past me and straight into the kitchen. Grandad Sykes follows her inside. He coughs in my face and stumbles through the door. He slowly shuffles over to Gran Sykes as she screams and yells into the garden. I can hear Grandad Sykes gasp and choke his way outside to the sounds of Gran Sykes' clicks and moans, treating him like a caged animal.

Grandad Sykes isn't far off Gran Sykes. A part from the fact his illnesses are genuine. He uses a walker because his legs are fucked and he can barely stand straight. This is down to several factors. He's severely overweight with a massive beer belly caused by years of eating greasy foods and sugar. Also, he carries around an oxygen tank to help him breathe after decades of smoking. He hasn't allowed his declining health to affect his actions. He still smokes like a chimney and eats crap food like it's Easter Sunday. He keeps several bags of sweets and packets of cigarettes resting next to his oxygen tank. Grandad Sykes swears more than Gran Sykes. Unlike Gran Sykes, he doesn't do it for attention. He does it because he's a retard with a minimal vocabulary and a very low IQ. Grandad Sykes has severe anger issues and used to be violent, which he can't follow up on these days.

Gran Sykes has a case of Munchausen syndrome by proxy. She loves the fact Grandad Sykes is declining in health and often brags about how well she takes care of him. She's told me for the past five Christmases that it would be his last before his heart gave out and he died. Gran Sykes laughs and smiles when she tells everybody she thinks he may have cancer. None of this is ever factual. Gran Sykes loves to be seen as the Florence Nightingale of her time. I'm confident she makes him sicker than he needs to be so that she can hold all of the power and attention.

Gran Sykes constantly posts on the internet about how Grandad Sykes' health affects her and what an outstanding person she is for caring for him and dealing with the suffering he brings her.

I hear Gran Sykes loudly swearing in the garden.

"Who the fuck is this daft cunt?"

I swiftly walk outside and see Mrs. Sykes sitting on a bench and drinking a glass of water with ice and lemon. Grandad Sykes has lit a cigarette and is pushing along the grass. Gran Sykes rushes over to Mr. Pyjamas, standing in the corner looking at the blazing sun and lightly combing his quiff. Gran Sykes is pointing directly into Mr. Pyjamas' face. I make my way over to the pair of them.

"Gran, this is Mr. Pyjamas."

"Mr. Pyjamas?"

"Yeah."

"What sort of name is that?"

"Err…"

"It's Italian, kid."

"What did he say?"

"He said it's Italian."

"He doesn't look Italian."

"Kid!"

"Yeah?"

"Who's this annoying bitch?"

"This is Gran Sykes."

"Eh? What did he say, the daft buggar?"

"He asked who this beautiful lady is?"

"Who asked?"

"Mr. Pyjamas asked."

"I am beautiful. He's right, even for a dirty Italian. I've seen what those bloody Italian fascists did to beautiful Malta."

Mr. Pyjamas stares at Gran Sykes with utter disgust. He put his pack of cigarettes and comb in his jacket. I can see a gun poking out of his leather trouser pocket. Gran Sykes begins to poke and tug at Mr Pyjamas. I glance upstairs at Baby Owl's bedroom window. I take deep breaths and try to take each moment as it comes.

"Come on, Gran. Let's get you a drink."

I gently grab Gran Sykes' shoulder and lead her away from Mr. Pyjamas.

"Mrs. Sykes is over there. Why don't you go speak to her?"

"I'm over here, Gran Sykes!"

"I can see yah. Daft slag!"

"Gran!"

"Sorry. I meant gorgeous Granddaughter in law. Is that better?"

"Go sit down, Gran."

"Fine."

Gran Sykes moans and groans her way across the grass. Grandad Sykes hasn't said a word. He's still smoking and gasping his way around the outside of the garden. The oxygen machine turned up to its total capacity. Me and Mrs. Sykes shout over to each other.

"Get Gran Sykes a drink, darl!"

"Punch?"

"No, no, not yet, not yet. I'll bring out the punch when everybody is here. It's a 'group thing.' Don't worry about serving anybody punch, darl. Leave that to me."

"Eh? What punch?"

"Nothing, Gran. Don't worry yourself."

"Don't tell me what to do."

"Right, sorry."

Gran Sykes sits next to Mrs. Sykes as she pours them a glass of wine. I nervously dash back to Mr. Pyjamas as he returns to his plastic chair in the corner. The corner without any shade or protection from the scorching sunshine.

"This ain't going to work, kid."

"What?"

"Trying to kill them all with a fucking drink."

"Why won't it?"

"I ain't giving you instructions. I've already given you enough. Look around you, kid. This is all a product of my giving. Give, give, give, that's all I do. Take, take, take, that's all you do. Now it's time for you to give back to me."

"We will, Mr. P, we will. I promise you. I don't see what's wrong with the poisoned punch idea?"

Mr. Pyjamas turns his back on me and mumbles to himself. He puts his hands on his head and stretches out in frustration. Eventually, he turns to face me.

"What's up, Mr. P?"

"Urgh…urgh…I appreciate that you're trying, kid. But I'm finding it hard to come down to your level of thinking. The poisoning idea is stupid, kid."

"Err, well, err, yeah, you're entitled to your opinion. I'll take that on board."

"Y'think everybody will take a perfectly timed sip and drop down dead, one after the other?"

"Well, yeah, kind of."

"Don't be a dumbass."

"Right."

"We ain't in a Scorsese mobster flick, kid."

"Obviously."

"Real life ain't like The Godfather."

Is this guy serious? I think he's being serious! The most stereotypical person I've met in my entire life doesn't appreciate cliches and genres. Yet, he's the one who has to come down to my level of thinking.

"The number of holes in your plan, kid."

"Such as?"

"When people don't get sick from the punch simultaneously, those who aren't getting sick will stop drinking when they see what happened to everybody else."

"Oh, err, well, yeah...That's your opinion…"

"As soon as the first person collapses, you're done, kid."

"Well, I'll think of something, Mr. P."

"Do you have a backup plan?"

"We do."

"You may want to consider using that."

"Do you plan on staying the entire evening?"

"Yep."

"Right."

Crack!

Crack!

Boom!

Boom!

The front door.

More guests. What if they wake Baby Owl? Why has nobody mentioned Baby Owl? The whole barbecue is a celebration of her, after all. Not a single question about our newborn.

Crack!

Crack!

Boom!

Boom!

The front door, again.

"I'm coming! I'm coming!"

Everybody stares at me.

"I'm going to answer it."

Jesus, it's so hot. I leave the garden and quickly remove my dark blue suit jacket. I drape it over one of our Brooklyn padded dining chairs with the blue diamond padded backs and roll up my white shirt sleeves.

I unlock the chains and bolts and pull the door wide open.

It's Mama Sykes and Uncle Sykes!

Mama Sykes is sitting in her wheelchair, with Uncle Sykes standing behind her and dripping in sweat. Mama Sykes and Uncle Sykes are siblings but look inbred. Mama Sykes lost her ability to walk after getting hit by an ice cream van while trying to figure out the difference between the red man and the green man crossing the road. Uncle Sykes is a mad conspiracy theorist who believes the Earth is flat, Jews run the world, there's no such thing as outer space, and the list goes on and on. With Mama Sykes' physical disabilities

and severe childlike stupidity, alongside Uncle Sykes'
conspiracy rantings, they make quite the pair.

"Hiya, Mr. Sykes."

"Hi, Mama Sykes."

"You've put on weight, Mr. Sykes."

"Thanks, Uncle Sykes."

"Anytime. So has Mama Sykes, haven't yah?"

"He's not stopped telling me the whole way here
how fat I am."

"Err, yep. Hmm. Do you both want to come
inside?"

"Who else is here?"

"Gran Sykes, Grandad Sykes, Mrs. Sykes, Mr.
Pyjamas, and the exceptional cutie pie Baby Owl."

"Who's that?"

"Baby Owl? That's the whole reason we're all here.
Baby Owl is mine, and Mrs. Sykes…"

"I'm not interested in that! Who's Mr. Pyjamas?"

"He's, err, he's just a family friend."

"Let me see him."

Uncle Sykes aggressively wheels Mama Sykes
across my foot and into the house. I hear the pair of them
racing to the back garden.

"Weeee!"

Mama Sykes pretends she's on a fairground ride
with her arms in the air. I carefully close the door behind
me. I can hear the garden erupting with noise. All of the
usual culprits. The Sykes family is swearing and

shouting across the garden. Vulgarity gives them an immense sense of power when amongst a group. I better help Mrs. Sykes. I've left her on duty to deal with them.

They're not allowed to drink the punch until I've given the go ahead.

I slowly breeze out into the boiling hot and verbally intense garden. Why have none of my family mentioned Baby Owl? That is the whole reason we seemingly arranged this gathering. Also, they have yet to ask how we are in such great shape. They haven't questioned how everything has significantly expanded to the grandest and most expensive standard possible. As I look around the garden, there's no concern or interest in anything concerning me and Mrs. Sykes. Just an obsession with Mr. Pyjamas, who they clearly see as a threat. The unknown man with the weird name is standing in the corner. My family is obsessed with the 'other.' The changes in our lives, even those of a highly metaphysical and bizarrely irrational nature, have slipped them by. Neither have they questioned the disappearances of Ravemachine, Sand Viper, Catholic Daddy, or The Son. They haven't been slightly concerned or worried. Maybe things will be different when Mrs. Sykes' family unit arrives. Perhaps they will have more to say regarding the reasoning behind the barbecue, our new looks and lives, and Baby Owl. If Baby Owl came downstairs, flew out of the kitchen window, around the garden, landed on their shoulders, and gave them loving pecks on their cheeks, they wouldn't bat an eyelid or show an ounce of interest. Only me, Mrs. Sykes, and Baby Owl share genuine love and care for one another.

"Mr. Sykes!"

"Yes, darl?"

"Can I have a word in the kitchen, please?"

"Yep."

Me and Mrs. Sykes walk into the kitchen, closing the door behind us as Mr. Pyjamas leans back in his chair and watches the bizarre Sykes family unwind into drunken vulgarity. Gran Sykes is on her third wine, Grandad Sykes his third bottle of beer, Uncle Sykes on his third whisky, and Mama Sykes is trying to open a packet of salted peanuts from the buffet. Me and Mrs. Sykes stand near the poisoned punch. I silently mix the liquids as the time ticks toward the final judgment. Mrs. Sykes' family members should be arriving soon.

"This isn't going to work."

"It was your idea, Mrs. Sykes."

"I know, but it's a stupid plan."

"It will work. We've got no other choice."

"Will you stop stirring the punch and look at me when I speak to you."

"Sorry, Mrs. Sykes."

I leave the bowl and concentrate on my wife.

"Your family is so crude and aggressive. Gran Sykes has tried to start three arguments with me."

"Go talk to somebody else."

"I did."

"Who?"

"Grandad Sykes. He said the word 'cunt' fifteen times during a conversation about the weather. Then Uncle Sykes tried to start an argument with Mr. Pyjamas, which I had to get in the middle of."

"Ah, shit."

"Yep."

"Well, your family should be arriving soon. We must keep them entertained for a short while, and then we can bring out the poisoned punch."

"What if it doesn't work?"

"Jesus Christ! That's what Mr. Pyjamas said."

"He's got a point."

"There are hundreds of crushed-up pills."

"It just doesn't sound right."

"But it sounded right when you came up with it?"

"That's not what I'm saying, Mr. Sykes."

I'll prove her and Mr. Pyjamas wrong when I serve up huge glasses of poisoned punch and watch them all drop like flies. Mr. Pyjamas can bag them all up and ride into the sunset with the bodies. Whatever it is that he does with our dead family corpses.

"I'm going to go check on Baby Owl. You can deal with your lot in the garden."

"Fine."

Mrs. Sykes leaves me in the kitchen. I go back to aggressively stirring the poisoned punch and adding more booze. I empty bottles of whisky, gin, vodka, and rum into the bowl. Paranoid that Mrs. Sykes and Mr. Pyjamas are right about the plan being a failure, I dash over to the sink, crouch down, open the drawer, and grab a massive bottle of bleach. I slide back over to the punch bowl, quickly undo the lid, empty the entire bottle of bleach into the poisoned punch, and mix it with the silver ladle like my life depended on it. I chuck the plastic bottle into the bin and grab some tinfoil which I wrap over the bowl. Mrs. Sykes is quiet, so I assume that Baby Owl is fine. I'll go upstairs in a bit and stroke her feathers.

Mr. Pyjamas breezes his way into the kitchen and slams the door.

"What is it, Mr. P?"

"I'm getting sick of waiting, kid. Y'think I ain't got other shit to do? But I've gotta sit in the scorching sun and listen to your hillbilly hicks. Time is ticking. Tick tock, tick tock. Remember what I told you? This is your final chance, kid."

"I know, mate, but we've planned it perfectly. I promise it won't be long. Mrs. Sykes' family should arrive soon, and everything will be done."

Mr. Pyjamas takes off his dark sunglasses and holds them in his hand. He slowly walks across the kitchen.

The sound of his leather thighs slapping together. His heels stamping against the hard floor. The almighty quiff bounces up and down, glowing like an angel sent from heaven. He walks slower and slower. Minutes have passed by the time he's towering over me. We've been in this situation before. Quite a few times. His colossal frame is leaning over me as his red eyes burn with satanic fire. I nod to let him know I'm aware of his constantly repeated threats. He puts his sunglasses back on. Mr. Pyjamas returns to his garden corner. I can hear my family singing eighties power ballads. I can't make out which songs they're screeching, but it sounds like Meatloaf or Bonnie Tyler.

Crack!

Crack!

Boom!

Boom!

"I'm coming!"

The music in the garden is getting louder since we left the Sykes family alone. This is precisely what happened after great aunt's funeral. It wasn't long before these filthy animals began to sing and scream like dirty, drunken pirates at sea.

Crack!

Crack!

Boom!

Boom!

"I'm coming!"

I race to the front door. Slipping and sliding in these expensive shoes on our state-of-the-art tiles.

I unlock the chains and bolts and pull the door wide open.

It's all of Mrs. Sykes' family unit!

Finally, it looks as though they've all come together.

Let me check.

We've got Jugs, Mark, Mommy, and Step Pappa.

I move out of the way so the group of sad cases can barge and squeeze their way into the house. I'm greeted with a unique and exciting introduction as each family member passes me. It's as though they're having a competition to see who can make me cringe the most.

Mrs. Sykes' sister Jugs is the first to walk into the gaff. She's roughly five-foot-tall with enormous size E boobs! Medical professionals recommended not to get such big bazookas as her tiny frame couldn't handle mega bags shoved into her body. So she had a dodgy backstreet operation in the city by some poorly qualified plastic surgeon. The boob bags haven't killed her yet, but they look ridiculous. The boob job has taken over her entire body and ripped through the skin, looking like they could burst any second.

Jugs is also a compulsive liar. She lies about everything, age, name, what she had for dinner last night, what she's doing during the day. The biggest lie is her accent. Jugs lived in Birmingham until she was twenty-one. Naturally, she speaks with a thick Brummie accent. Instead, she manipulates her voice to sound heightened RP. Like a member of the Royal Family, she insists on respect like multigenerational royalty.

"Hello, Mr. Sykes! Mwah, mwah. Great to see you again, darling. Odoo is fabulous. I see you've dressed up too."

"Err, yep. Hi, err, Jugs..."

Jugs barges past me and clicks after her husband, Mark. Mark is in the Royal Navy, which is how the pair met. He's a trained weapons specialist, and considering how stupid Mark is, I doubt he will ever be allowed to use a weapon. He's ten years younger than Jugs and looks like he's just left school. He's lanky, spotty, and can barely speak. He's essentially Jugs' servant. Jugs clicks at Mark, who follows without saying a word.

Finally, we have Mrs. Sykes' Mommy and Step Pappa. A couple of wheeler dealers. They don't earn money through work but through dodgy dealings. They will sell pyramid schemes, knock-off goods, stolen cars, you name it. Step Pappa has four golden teeth and used to live in a caravan by the sea. Mommy is the epitome of mutton dressed as lamb. She's fifty-seven but tries to dress as though she's Jugs and Mrs. Sykes' age. Mommy tried to follow in Jugs' footsteps and got a boob job. But she managed to stay within her body range and got a C size. Mommy has nice round boobs. Jugs' are so big they've turned into the shape of traffic cones. She also followed in Step Pappa's footsteps and got a couple of gold teeth. The couple are already drunk and holding cans of strong lager.

"Whey! Good to see you, Mr. Sykes."

"You too, Mommy."

"It's been a long time."

"Everybody is already in the garden, Mommy."

"Bring it on!"

Mommy barges past and spills disgusting beer onto my clean shirt.

"Y'alright, geezer?"

"How are you doing, Step Pappa?"

"Y'know, fella, a bit of this, a bit of that."

"Yeah."

"Got any johnnies?"

"What?"

"Condoms? Rubbers?"

"I don't."

"Ah! Fuck's sake, mate."

"Sorry."

"Me and Mommy fancied a wet and sloppy fuck upstairs."

"Hmm."

"No worries, geezer. We'll do it in the garden if we have to."

Step Pappa barges past me and into the kitchen. I close the front door and shake my head. Both families are drinking, smoking, and singing in the garden.

Mr. Pyjamas walks into the house and stares at me across the kitchen.

"It's time, kid! I've waited long enough. I want their bodies, now."

I nod at Mr. Pyjamas as he pushes into the front room. I peek around the door. He's lying on the expensive sofa and smoking a cigarette.

I run up two flights of stairs into Baby Owl's bedroom. Mrs. Sykes is sitting in a chair next to Baby Owl's cot. She puts her finger over her lips and tells me to be quiet. I mouth the words 'Go time, go time,' which means time for us to use the poisoned punch. Mrs. Sykes holds Baby Owl and refuses to come downstairs.

It's up to me to do this by myself.

I sprint downstairs, down the hall, through the kitchen, and into the scorching hot garden. Don't worry, Mrs. Sykes and Baby Owl. Daddy is coming to save you both.

Let the poisoning commence.

I undo three shirt buttons so that my chest hair is showing, mainly because of the heat. My expensive shoes and black trousers are tightly done up. I take off my gold watch and ram it into my pocket. I walk into the kitchen and lift the tinfoil on top of the poisoned punch. It fucking stinks. I take out red foam cups and grab a silver ladle, planning to fill each cup with punch. I place both on the kitchen side. I open the back door and enter the garden holding the bowl with both hands. As I go from the kitchen to the outdoor table, I see what looks like the last days of Rome. I manage to travel across the sweltering hot garden and place it on the table. My next action plan is to return inside, grab the cups, and silver ladle, propose a toast, and get everybody to gulp the poisoned punch.

I look around and am disgusted at what I see.

Gran Sykes is standing next to Mommy, who has so much fake tan on her face that she looks like a bloated carrot. They're both knocking back tequila slammers and gossiping about how much weight me and Mrs. Sykes have put on. Not a single mention of poor Baby Owl. They lick the salt off their hands, down the tequila, and squirt the lemon into their mouths. They both let out the screeching and shrieking that sends shivers down your spine.

I glance across the garden and see Jugs with her colossal boobs hanging from her bra, dangling for everybody to see. Nobody is batting an eyelid. She's got giant nipples like salami slices with grapes in the centre. Jugs is quickly knocking back shot after shot of Sambuca. Her Navy partner Mark has a dog collar around his neck and is being walked around the garden on his hands and knees. Jugs whacks him with his lead as he barks and yelps. Mark downs a shot of Sambuca from Jugs' cleavage as a reward. Mark seems to enjoy staying in character as a whipped doggy as Jugs crouches down to his level and breastfeeds him like a baby. Mark sucks on Jugs' massive boobs and cries out like an infant. They move around the garden and attempt to grab everybody's attention.

Nobody cares about them.

Nobody answers.

As I walk back inside, I see Uncle Sykes and Step Pappa drinking cans of lager and talking about how the moon landing was fake and how JFK isn't dead. They're screaming and shouting at each other. It's the loudest conversation I've ever heard.

Grandad Sykes and Mama Sykes are sitting on the edges. Occasionally, one of them pipes up with a question or comment while watching the rest of the barbecue unfold, as they're too sick to get involved in booze, dancing, fetishism, and conspiracy theories.

Mama Sykes sits quietly on her phone, drooling and playing a game of Snake. She knows nothing of the world. I've often imagined tipping her out of her wheelchair into the road and refusing to help until she could answer one of my simple questions. Such as 'two plus two.'

I shake my head and dash back into the kitchen. Mr. Pyjamas was right. Our family units need to go as quickly as possible. I stack the red foam cups and grab everything I need to serve my homemade poisoned punch.

I hear music blasting from the garden. Gran Sykes, Mommy, Jugs, Mark, Uncle Sykes, and Step Pappa roll on the grass to the music. It isn't hippie music, but songs from the eighties. They're sprawled across the grass and singing their hearts out.

I look around the garden for Mama Sykes, and she's accidentally wheeled herself towards the buffet table. I begin to panic as I notice her reach for the poisoned punch. Everybody is too engrossed in their bubbles to notice or care about Mama Sykes. Mama Sykes reaches forward from her wheelchair and rams loads of the buffet food into her little mouth. I assume the smell from the poisoned punch will put her off. But it doesn't. She looks around to see who's watching her. Nobody. She fills up her Mr Men's child's mug with some punch and gulps it. I drop the red foam cups and silver ladle onto the hard kitchen floor. I run outside and sprint across the garden to the buffet table, slapping the Mr Men's child's mug out of Mama Sykes' hand.

"Mama Sykes!"

"Argh, my drink."

"That wasn't for you, Mama Sykes. We were supposed to be having a toast together. Remember? Did you drink a full mug of the punch?"

Mama Sykes nods her head.

The singing and music stops.

Everybody stares at me.

There's nowhere left to turn.

I'm trapped in a circle with nowhere to go.

I turn toward the kitchen door and see Mr. Pyjamas storm outside. He aggressively pulls out his pistol and begins to fire golden bullets. I drop to the grass and roll under the table.

WOOSH!

BANG!

WOOSH!
BANG!

WOOSH!

BANG!

WOOSH!

BANG!

WOOSH!

BANG!

WOOSH!

BANG!

WOOSH!

BANG!

WOOSH!

BANG!

I must have passed out because when I open my eyes, theirs a shining silver saviour in my face. I turn onto my back and look upwards. The sun glazing down into my eyes. I squint and see a figure. Dressed in all black. I roll onto my front and cough up blood. I try to push off the grass and stand up. But I can't. The figure in black crouches down to me. I turn around and look up.

"Mr. P?"
"It's me, darl."
"Mrs. Sykes?"
"Yeah."
"Baby Owl!"
"She's fine."

Mrs. Sykes gently strokes my head. She's sitting down on the grass next to me. The sun is getting hotter, and I'm sweating profusely. I don't say anything, stick my head on Mrs. Sykes' lap, and enjoy her rubbing my hair. Blood starts to drip from my forehead and onto her knee. After a while, I can't take the pain and heat any longer, so I sit up and look toward Mrs. Sykes.

I see Mr. Pyjamas in his all-black leather biker outfit. His sunglasses and huge quiff combed over his head. He's not sweating or shaking. I stare at him. He's holding the shining silver saviour to the back of Mrs. Sykes' head. Her eyes are watering. She's crying. I've only just noticed her hands trembling. She looks terrified and like she's going to collapse. Me and Mrs. Sykes both stand up. Mr. Pyjamas nods at Mrs. Sykes. She quietly tiptoes back into the kitchen, stepping over our family's dead bodies and screeching in fear under her breath. She stumbles back indoors. It takes her some time. I hear Mrs. Sykes collapse onto the hard kitchen floor. I'm standing in just my boxer shorts which are smothered in blood. Sweat dribbles into my eyes. I wipe away the sweat and look at an all-blackened Mr. Pyjamas. He points the shining silver saviour right in between my eyes.

Neither of us moves or says a word. I struggle to see, and my legs can barely hold my weight. My head feels like it could explode.

"What, err, what now, Mr. P?"

My throat is so dry that I can barely get my words out.

"Pack your bag."

I cough and spit out sounds.

"Pack a bag. You're both coming with me."

I stagger and stumble across the garden with Mr. Pyjamas pointing his pistol at the back of my head.

Finally, we reach the kitchen door. I turn around to speak to Mr. Pyjamas.

"A bag?"

"It won't take long, kid. You don't need much where you're going."

CHAPTER 7

I sprint back to our flat and unlock this shit piece of wood. He's expecting me, and I'm late. The handle breaks off. I throw it onto the cracked tiles and slam the door behind me.

"Stop panicking. I'm back!"

He must have been so worried about me. I run up the stairs as fast as possible and unlock and barge through this second door.

"I'm sorry I'm late, my good man."

Special Enforcer is leaning back in his chair. He's smoking a cigarette, still dressed in his all-white women's jumpsuit, white baseball cap with the words 'Special Enforcer' in big black letters, his white face mask, which he has pulled over his thick beard and down over his chin so that he can smoke, his white shoes that look like women's heels. Still, he insists they aren't, and bright purple lipstick smudges all over the end of his cigarette. We stare at each other as a chilling silence travels through the freezing-cold flat.

"He's in the bedroom. He'll be waiting for you."

Special Enforcer pipes up in his East End accent. I think he's from Bethnal Green or Bow or another one of London's dead and collapsed working-class areas.

"Hopefully, you're not too pissed off that I'm late?"

"You don't need to worry about what I think. He's the one who's paying."

"I've gotten everything you asked me to."

"Tell him."

"I got your favourite, mate!"

I shout to him from the kitchen. The whole flat shakes as I scream that loud.

"Better get to work. I'm not paying you to be a lazy prick."

Special Enforcer sits there, smoking his cigarette and playing with his face mask.

I frantically drop the plastic bags onto the table.

"I picked up what he asked. Wait for it! Drum roll…drum roll…drum roll…Jam! Jars and jars of jam. Just for him."

I lift one jar after another, after another, after another, onto the table. There must be at least twenty jars of jam. The table gets wholly covered in jars. I've spoilt him, spoilt him rotten. Special Enforcer sticks his thumbs up and blows me a kiss with his sparkling purple lips. Letting me know I've done an excellent job.

"I knew you'd be happy. That's not all I've got either."

I pick up the other bag and put it on the side. There's no room left on the table.

"Beans! Tins and tins of beans, just for you."

"How many more times? This isn't for me."

"No, err, I didn't mean it like that."

"He's the one paying me for this. I'm the one paying you."

"I didn't mean…."

"I don't care. Jam and beans aren't my thing."

"No worries."

I cover the entire kitchen side in tins of beans. There must be at least thirty tins. There's enough jam and beans to last us. It would probably survive a nuclear apocalypse. That's undoubtedly next. First, the breakdown of society. Finally, we'll have a complete breakdown of the planet. People like him in the bedroom won't give a shit. He's old enough not to be around for any of it. He's got jam and beans and old age.

"He's excited."

"Err, is he?"

"Sure."

"It's not for me to judge."

"If this is a man's dying wish, an experience he's willing to put his life savings into, something he's wanted to try his entire life but couldn't because of society fucking prejudice, who are we to judge?"

"Fair enough."

"He's paying top dollar for this."

"I couldn't believe it when you told me."

"He's spending his entire life savings."

"Doesn't he have, y'know, any family or friends?"

"Nah."

"I see."

"He's the kind of person they pick up. Men or women. Old cunts, who have a shit-ton of cash, no family, no friends, don't know what to do. So they sign up, and we get to work. Do you want to know what he said to me?"

"What?"

"He told me he was as giddy and excited as when he first lost his virginity as a teenager. He told me he lost it to a girl he had taken to the school disco."

"Jesus, how long ago was this?"

"He didn't say. So I'm thinking, maybe, fifty or sixty years ago."

"He's old, mate. Are you sure he'll still be able to get it up?"

"That's what the Prick Pill is for."

Special Enforcer is twisting his stubble between his fingers. He plays with his white face mask, lights another cigarette, and stares out the flat window. I begin to quickly and manically twist and rip the lids. He's reticent in the bedroom. I can't help but watch Special Enforcer click the back of his shoes on the wooden floorboards. His smooth, shaven legs and thick ankles attract my attention.

"He ain't saying much. I've got his favourite. This stock wasn't cheap. He could be a bit more grateful."

"Go talk to him. But don't fuck things up."

I leave the kitchen and go into the bedroom. The lazy bugger is just lying there.

"Hi, sir. Remember me? I'll be your host this evening. Along with Special Enforcer, who I believe collected you from your residence?"

He says nothing. Moody twat. After all I've done for him. He has the cheek to lie there, naked, with a big erection, smelling like crap. That isn't gratitude. I spent hours getting him food, ages picking up clothes, collecting candles for him, matches to light the candles, and the list goes on and on. The jam and beans aren't satisfying or gratifying him. I kind of knew that they wouldn't. I'd like a bit more appreciation for all that I do. I'm always the one who cleans up the stains and blood and vomit afterward. Urgh! He stinks, mate.

"Haven't you washed today, sir? Everybody needs a good wash."

The moody git says nothing. Some wealthy, old, polite paying customer he's turning out to be. I guess he's old and has to work a lot harder. You've got to work at life. Nothing good comes naturally.

"I'll be in the kitchen if you need me, sir. You're safe in here. Oh! Remember, if you need something to eat, the kitchen has the jam and beans you requested."

"Time?"

"Sorry?"

"Time…is it…here?"

"What time are we going to start, sir?"

"Hmm."

"As soon as I've finished putting the spread out in the kitchen."

"Now. Want it now!"

"We can't bring him now, sir."

"Hard."

"I know you're hard, sir, but…"

"Now!"

"Just a minute, sir. I'll see what I can do."

I close the bedroom door and walk into the front room.

"He wants the body right now. The Prick Pill is already working."

"Tell him that we can't do it right now."

"Can't you tell him?"

"I'm paying you to do this kind of shit. How many more times? This is your job. Mine is to organise everything and bring everybody together."

"Fuck's sake."

"Do it."

"Why can't we do it right now, again?"

"My Youngling needs time to unwrap the body. Once he's got the body ready, the three of us can take it into the bedroom. If he can't wait, we could get My Youngling to wank him off until the body is fully prepared and ready to go. Then he can do whatever he wants."

"What does he want to do?"

"Do you really want to know?"

"Err, yeah, well, I think so."

"He's paid for headless…"

"Urgh!"

"You asked."

"No, no, no. I do want to know. It just makes me feel sick."

"There's a bottle of rum on the side. Get yourself a drink."

I snatch the bottle of rum from the side, click it up, and then down a quarter of the bottle into my mush.

"Wow! Leave some for me."

I hand Special Enforcer the bottle of rum. He sits in his chair, downs the bottle, and lights another cigarette. I don't know why he's wearing his white mask. He keeps it around his chin while he smokes cigarette after cigarette. He looks ridiculous. Don't get me started on the white jumpsuit. My head starts to hurt. I can feel a pulsing sensation on both sides. I know what I need to do. I grab an empty jar and fill it full of black and lumpy sewage water, dripping from the tap when you turn it on. It stinks. I swig down the sewage water in one.

"That's messed up."

I can already feel the difference. When I lived with Mrs. Sykes, she always drank about four or five litres of water daily. She would always encourage me to do the same. No matter what the condition of the water was like.

"Ready, mate?"

"Yes."

"Where was I?"

"He's paid for headless…"

"Yeah! He's paid for the most expensive package on the dark web. The headless experience."

"What does that entail?"

"You've never done a headless while working for me?"

"Never."

"This is your first time?"

"Yep."

"Oh, shit! No wonder you're so goddamn scared."

"Exactly."

"My Youngling will unwrap the corpse."

"I know the drill."

"His head will have been cut off beforehand."

"Right, well…"

"People could easily cut a head to pieces if they wanted to. They don't cost much money, not in the grand scheme. That's why you and My Youngling are my hand-picked workers. That's why you're second in line. If anything ever happens to me, you'll take over as leader of this operation. If anything happens to you, then My Youngling will take over. Understand?"

"Yes."

"Good. Now, where was I?"

"Headless."

"Boom! We'll bring him upstairs, drag his body into the bedroom, close the door, let the old geezer do what he needs to do, y'know, same as always, mate. Just with no head this time around."

"But we all get paid more money?"

"We sure do mate."

"How much more?"

"Triple!"

"Triple?"

"Yep."

"That means I can send triple the amount back to Mrs. Sykes and Baby Owl?"

"It sure as hell does."

"Right. OK. I'm up for anything if this is for my family. Where do you want me?"

"Go back in there and explain that he'll have to wait longer. Maybe twenty to thirty minutes."

"Will do, mate."

It's half an hour later. Everything is set up in its place. Since I did a lot of the heavy lifting, so to speak, Special Enforcer gave me a break. A chance to sober up and rest. Special Enforcer and My Youngling have taken the headless, decayed, rotten corpse into the bedroom. They've both returned from cleaning the outside area and ensuring no traces are left behind. I lead My Youngling up the stairs as we wait for the old geezer to do what he needs to do.

He's paying all of his life savings to the company that Special Enforcer works for. They're a huge company that operates across the country, which was created and is run by Mr. Pyjamas. Mr. Pyjamas' company can be tracked down via the dark web. He provides self-services to old, dying pensioners with no family to leave their expenses to. The old geezers are generally very rich and have been tracked down in old people's homes or housing residences. Sometimes even in a hospice. The whole financial exchange and all the contractual obligations can occur over the dark web. It's pretty simple. The rich, old, lonely, dying pervert will have endless sexual options to choose from. One of the most popular services lately is sex with a corpse. This is why Mr. Pyjamas collects dead bodies from many scared and blackmailed acquaintances. He uses bribes, threats, and violence to provide the sexual desires of the high-paying customer. Eventually implemented into his company and earned a lot of money.

Special Enforcer will set up the whole shebang in the flat. Mr. Pyjamas' company gets paid, and Special Enforcer gets his cut. Me and My Youngling are working under Special Enforcer, so we both get a cut.

Special Enforcer needs us both. Sales and production have gone through the roof. Word has spread throughout the dark web. The company is getting so popular that Mr. Pyjamas is about to open several new branches. Not just for rich, old, dying perverts. But for perverts of all races, genders, ages, shapes, and sizes. He doesn't discriminate. Mr. Pyjamas believes in diversity, equity, and inclusion when it comes to the dark sexual fantasies of everybody. True freedom. Right?

Since I started working under Special Enforcer a couple of months ago, I've only seen corpses that still have heads. So this will be my first experience dealing with a headless body. Special Enforcer has come through and paid me a massive chunk of what he earned from the sexual experiences. This time we're all getting paid triple! This means Mrs. Sykes and Baby Owl will get paid triple. I really need to get down to some serious hard graft. Everything I've done or will ever do is for them. It doesn't matter if they love or hate me. Even if working for Mr. Pyjamas eradicates all my morals and crushes my values.

I open the door and calmly lead Special Enforcer up the stairs and into the flat. His white heels clicking and clacking on the solid wood as he sluggishly limps. He has his white mask covering his mouth. His ripped biceps and solid pecks hang out of his white jumpsuit.

He's carrying his white cap in his left hand, clinging onto it for dear life. I know how stressful cleaning up all of the mess can be. It gets even worse cleaning up afterward.

"Come in, come in, mate. Make yourself comfortable and relaxed. We still have jam and beans if you're hungry or have the munchies. The old, ungrateful twat in the bedroom hasn't touched any of it."

"What the hell is going on in there?"

"He wanted some music playing in the bedroom while he got to business. So I whacked it on from my phone. If you fancy a boogie, we can have a little dance."

"It sounds like music from a hundred years ago."

"It is. Well, pretty much. It's the song he and his wife first made love to. Also, the last song they made love to just before she died."

"Why are you so fucking happy?"

"We're getting paid triple! Y'know how much triple will help Mrs. Sykes in the village? A lot. More than a lot. Also, I've found some of my old emotion suppression tablets. The ones I had to take when I first started working here. They were in the front pocket of my rucksack. If we mix them with booze, it will get the three of us smashed. The three of us can all take some later. We'll each take six to get us going. I've rambled on long enough. Sit down, mate."

I get some chairs huddled together for my boys. We all sit together in a circle. I look to my right. My Youngling is sitting next to me. He looks so young. He can't be older than fourteen.

"How old are you again, mate?"

He doesn't answer me. He looks scared. His lip is quivering as though he's about to cry. I thought he was meant to have balls of steel. He's got even more experience than me with corpses. They must be tears of joy.

"It's alright, My Youngling. I'll get emotional afterward, too. We all will. My wife and kid are probably crying at home right now, wondering when I will send the next bit of digital currency. My Youngling! That reminds me, you and the old geezer should meet. I know you saw him when you dropped his body on the bed. But I mean properly. An actual conversation. He's going to love you. He was cold as ice with me at first, Special Enforcer too. But once you talk to him, he's a really nice guy. He knows a lot about music. We spoke about Mozart and Bach."

My Youngling is very quiet. Shivering and shaking in his chair.

"How old are you, mate?"

He refuses to answer my question. I knew Special Enforcer shouldn't have taken him on. It should just be me working for him. My Youngling leans over the chair and vomits all over the floor. My Youngling is choking, retching, and sick everywhere. It stinks. It reminds me of when Mrs. Sykes used to throw up during her pregnancy.

"It must be something you ate. Or a bug that's going around."

I gesture for My Youngling to get all his vomit onto the floor.

"Do you want me to ask him?"

Special Enforcer finally pipes up in his thick Cockney accent. He finally offers to talk some sense into him. What a generous bloke. He's sat on my left side and doing his usual. He pulls his white mask over his chin, takes out his purple lipstick, and smears it all over his plump lips, then smokes cigarette after cigarette, playing with his cap and flexing those huge ripped muscles. Special Enforcer claims he hasn't had a lip job. But it sure as hell looks like he's had one.

"Thanks, mate."

"Just let me finish my cigarette, mate."

We both sit and wait while Special Enforcer smokes his cigarette. He leans back in his chair and stares out of the flat window. My Youngling is still retching up all of his nerves.

"This is a great tune! I can understand why he's playing it over and over and over and over again. It must turn him on. The Prick Pill should last a couple of hours. After that, who knows how many rounds he's got with the body."

My Youngling stops retching. Special Enforcer finishes smoking and stands up. He's so ripped! His arms and chest are massive. Veins are popping out of his biceps. They look like they've got individual heartbeats and personalities. He confidently swaggers and prances in his girly jumpsuit towards My Youngling. I look at the pair, and Special Enforcer lowers himself onto his knees.

"Look, mate, you haven't got anything to worry about. We both have your best interest at heart. Don't we?"

"Yeah, mate, we're here for you, My Youngling. Just relax."

My Youngling starts to calm down. Well, he stops shaking. Special Enforcer tries to bring peace to the flat in his East End twang. I understand this kind of work can make you emotional. But My Youngling has seen and done much worse to be recruited in the first place. I know that I have.

"You've got us. We're here for you no matter what."

My Youngling nods his head and gets himself together. He stops crying. Special Enforcer kisses him on the cheek, which leaves a big purple lipstick mark on My Youngling. He goes to wipe the lipstick mark from his cheek. Special Enforcer tightly grabs hold of My Youngling's fingers.

"Don't you dare wipe that kiss mark."

"Argh! I Sorry, sorry, sorry."

"Understand?"

"Argh! Yes, yes, yes."

"Good."

Special Enforcer lets go of My Youngling's fingers. He grabs his head and kisses him on the other cheek, which leaves an even bigger and brighter purple lipstick mark. Special Enforcer pushes himself up from the floor. His mask nearly falls off his face as he rubs his grizzly stubble with his massive hands. He manages to get up to his feet. He looks physically worn out. Poor guy. Special Enforcer grabs another cigarette, lights it, and returns to his seat. My Youngling nurses his seemingly broken fingers.

"How old are you, My Youngling?"

My Youngling stutters and tries to get his words out. He nurses his hand and begins to cry.

"I'm, err, I'm, err, I'm ten years old, Mr. Sykes."

"Nine?"

"Yes."

"What the fuck do you mean?"

"My age."

I jump out of my seat and stare at Special Enforcer.

"Is this true?"

"I thought you knew, mate."

"Nine!"

"It's not a big deal. My Youngling has been helping out in this for years."

"How the hell does that work?"

"Tell him, My Youngling."

"My brothers."

"His brothers used to work for the company. Five or six years. My Youngling helped them out from the start until they were killed, Mr Pyjamas kept him on, and that's when we met."

"Five or six years? So you've been doing this since you were four years old?"

"Hmm."

"That's messed up, Special Enforcer."

"Chill out."

My Youngling stops moving and stares at the floor.

"Make yourself useful, Mr Sykes. Go into the bedroom and check on the old geezer."

"Fine. Will do."

I huff and puff my way into the bedroom. I expect to see him sitting up in bed, music blasting, having a wank with his eyes closed. But he isn't. He's just lying there. The room stinks, that's for sure. It stinks.

Urgh!

Fuck!

Jesus Christ!

The old geezer is dead!

I crack open a window as I'm struggling to breathe.

I can't help but focus on the headless corpse.

Rotting, dirty, rancid, damp, rank, bleeding, smelly, evil-smelling, stinking flow of blood, outpouring, grieving, agonising, aching, heartbreak...

ARGH!

ARGH!

ARGH!

I hear loud bangs and screams coming from the front room.

I sprint out of the bedroom and through the kitchen.

"What the hell was that?"

I look down, and My Youngling is lying on the floor.

He's drenched in rivers of blood.

My Youngling is dead.

Special Enforcer is sitting in his chair. He's staring out of the window and flexing his arms. The sun lights up his white jumpsuit and muscles to make him look like a Greek god.

I sit down and stare at Special Enforcer.

"What the hell happened?"

"He did it to himself, mate. I was sitting here, smoking my cigarette, playing with my cap. Next thing, he pulls his Stanley knife out of his pocket. I thought he was coming at me, so I pulled out my Stanley knife, and he turned his blade on himself. Cut his own throat."

"Shit! Shit! Shit!"

"It isn't that bad. Now you can have more responsibility and more money for your family."

"It's not just My Youngling who's dead."

"Don't tell me..."

"Yep. The geezer's dead too."

"Bastard…"

Special Enforcer jumps out of his chair and points at me to sit down.

"Just sit down and shut your mouth, alright?"

"What do we do?"

"Let me think, let me think, let me think."

Special Enforcer paces around the flat to avoid My Youngling's body. He tries not to stand in his blood, not to touch or look at him. A glowing Special Enforcer lights himself another cigarette, throws his white mask and cap onto the bloodied floor, and stares in horror at what he's allowed to happen. I was only gone a couple of minutes.

"If the old geezer ain't alive when the Informers come here to pick him up, we don't get paid. The rule is we have to return an alive and satisfied customer. I have to agree and sign every time I take on work for Mr. Pyjamas. If he ain't breathing, Mr. P ain't paying."

Special Enforcer throws his cigarette to the red-stained floor and stands on it. He tries to zip up his jumpsuit, but he's damaged it too much, stretched the cotton, and started making holes. I don't have a clue what he's thinking.

I begin to notice his head travel in a particular direction. At first, I thought he was looking at My Youngling's dead body. Then, it seems he's just self-conscious about the blood on his white clothes, which must be expensive. Especially those clickety-clack heels. My gaze travels along the floor and rivers and rivers of blood flow. I stare at the dead body. I notice something. If My Youngling had slit his own throat, where was the knife? I scan along the floor and can't see My Youngling's knife.

"Where's the knife?"

"I've not got fucking time for this."

"I'm just asking."

"I don't pay you to ask."

"Fair enough."

"Maybe it's underneath his body or something."

I go over to My Youngling and expect to find a knife.

"What are you doing?"

"Getting the knife for you."

"Don't touch him!"

"Why?"

"What have I told you about questions?"

"It's not what you pay me for."

"Exactly. Idiot. Don't touch anything and get fingerprints on the body. Get us both into even more trouble. I'll do the heavy lifting. I've already had one little twat get us into trouble today."

I take a final look at My Youngling and notice he's lying on his back with his head pointing toward Special Enforcer and not away from him. The position he's lying in looks as though his throat was cut from the back. After a couple of minutes of silence, I finally pipe up.

"It was you. You killed My Youngling. Why? You said he was your second main man. Were you going to slash me too?"

"I've given you everything, Mr Sykes."

Special Enforcer nervously stares at the wooden floor.

"Hmm."

"My life was in danger."

"Danger from who?"

"Listen, I owe Mr. Pyjamas money, mate. A lot of money. These jobs haven't been about getting paid. They've been about paying off my debts to him. I've had to do whatever he's asked. Come on, mate. Do you know what it's like? Doing anything to save your life, or even worse, those you love. I slit My Youngling's throat so that it looked like an accident."

"You're right, mate. I can relate to you. Me and my wife killed both of our families to keep our daughter safe. I want to help you. Help us still get paid. We're in similar situations, Special Enforcer. I've got to pay off debts for Mrs. Sykes and Baby Owl. I owe Mr. Pyjamas too."

"Thanks, mate. I love you, my brother."

"You've never called me your brother before."

"We need to drag the two bodies over there. We'll put My Youngling and the geezer in the corner underneath with all of the bin bags. I'll hide their bodies and tell the Informers that My Youngling killed the geezer, and I killed My Youngling. We both say that it was self-defence. My Youngling pulled the knife to my neck. So, I stabbed him. It was to protect myself from a violent attack. Save the business and ensure the geezer or corpse wasn't damaged too much."

"Right, let's do this."

"When are they coming?"

"When I call and say the geezer is finished. It should give us enough time to get everything ready. I'm glad that he's gone. My Youngling got what he deserved in the end."

Special Enforcer goes back into the front room to make the call. He returns to the kitchen a couple of minutes later.

"I said the geezer was waiting for them. They should be here soon. We need to clean this place up, mate. Get to work, you little prick."

"Will do."

I run around the kitchen to sweep the mess from the table and have a quick spray to eliminate the smell of dead bodies.

Whatever I need to do to keep Mrs. Sykes and Baby Owl safe.

CHAPTER 8

An hour later, they're here.

First, they're banging at the piece of shit downstairs door. Then, before me and Special Enforcer have time to move, they start shouting from the street up to our window.

"Oi! Are you there?"

Special Enforcer rushes over to the window and bangs on the glass.

"We're here! Just a minute."

Special Enforcer points me towards the door.

"Go let the Informers into the flat."

I check my appearance in the window reflection. My plain grey jumper, black trousers, and black shoes look perfectly presentable. As I study how I look, Special Enforcer tries to cover up the rips in his white jumpsuit and adds another layer of sparkling purple lipstick. I leave him to it.

I hesitantly leave the flat, nervously go downstairs to answer the door, and let in the Informers. I grip the shitty handle and pull it open. It's the same fools as last time. Since we started working under Special Enforcer, Mr. Pyjamas sends three of his Informers monthly to check on us. All three Informers look identical. They're entirely bald. Imagine a white Buddhist monk having a baby with one of the Kray Twins. The three of them are roughly in their forties and five-foot-ten. Big black bushy beards which look like they need a good comb. They're wearing white robes from head to toe, as though they've come from the Roman Colosseum, with their tiny nipples and hairy chests showing. Their arms are covered in tattoos, and golden coin rings on every finger. All three are wearing bright red lipstick and white stiletto heels.

"Y'right, boys. Come in, come in."

"It's good to see you again, Mr. Sykes."

All three speak in unison with an even thicker Cockney accent than Special Enforcer. Almost swallowing their words as they spit them out.

"It's good to see you all."

I show these geezer-monk-drag queen Informers up to the flat.

"Watch your heels on the stairs. We've got cracks and holes in the wood. Special Enforcer is always getting his heel jammed in the hole."

"Thanks for the warning."

They all habitually speak in unison, like a Bethnal Green Church choir. But unfortunately, the sound gets all muffled through their hefty beards. I lead the Informers into the flat and dash into the kitchen to grab some chairs. I look over my shoulder, and the Informers have already got their screens out, taking notes and looking around the flat. Not a single body or piece of evidence has been handed to them. Yet they take it upon themselves to start being nosey straight away.

"Special Enforcer will be out soon. He's just in the bedroom wrapping everything up."

"We should think so."

I pick up three chairs and carry them into the room.

"There you go, boys."

"Can we take a look in the kitchen?"

"Err, I'll have to ask, err, I mean, yes, yes, you can."

The bald bastards start taking notes and rating the kitchen. I thought Special Enforcer had sharp heels, but these three are smashing the floor to pieces and stomping throughout the kitchen. I'd spent ages getting rid of the mess created and left behind by My Youngling. This chorus of Cockneys is clicking their heels like they're on a hen night.

I'd put those three chairs out for them. The ungrateful cretins. I can hear the Buddhist puffs clicking and typing away on their pads. Where the hell is Special Enforcer? This is the first time I've dealt with Mr. Pyjamas' Informers for this long. Usually, it's a simple handshake, I leave to do my assigned job, and they deal with Special Enforcer. They definitely preferred My Youngling to me. His brothers were the company's top workers. My Youngling's family are the ones who made Mr. Pyjamas so financially successful. They provided the links and did all of the hard work that nobody else wanted to do, like collecting bodies. But ultimately, My Youngling's brothers betrayed Mr. Pyjamas' company and were killed. Their bodies were sold to be used as sexual objects to the very pensioners they had brought into the fold as rich and valuable customers.

I often daydream about my and Mrs. Sykes' families. Primarily upon hearing of the connection and sense of loss people feel when a loved one dies…

The Informers are in the kitchen and speaking amongst themselves. I look over. They're having a fierce debate over what's happened. I can hear muffles and grunts. They all light up their cigarettes and smoke, so I leave them to it. After they've finished nattering, which sounded like prostitutes arguing over who could have the best street corner, the only sounds are their fingers tapping on screens and the occasional sound of a drag on their cigarette or a click-click on the wood. I sit and chill in the front room. Waiting for Special Enforcer. Best get them out of here as soon as possible. I hear the Informers leave the kitchen. They move around and quickly rate-check the whole flat. It's tiny, so it should only take a little time. Finally, the Informers come back over to me with their heads lowered. Like they're delivering me bad news.

"Can you get Special Enforcer for us? We've seen everything that we need to in terms of the inspection."

"No worries."

All the Informers flex their muscles, one after the other, and they're even more ripped than Special Enforcer. They clench their massive fists to make their gold rings glow. They look like pirates who have just set sail to sea after finding treasure on a remote island. I understand the subtle threats of violence. I look down at their blood-covered white stiletto heels. I couldn't get rid of all the stains. As I go to the bedroom, I see all the cigarette butts they've thrown on the floor and covered in bright red lipstick. I can't wait for this to all be over. The Informers shake their heads at me in disgust as I leave the front room, walk into the bedroom, and close the door.

"Special Enforcer? The Informers need you. I can't stand them. The toilet-rimming, STD-ridden, germ-infested imbeciles. That's right. I know the word imbecile. Just get out there and do your thing, mate. Get them to piss off and leave us to it. We're knackered. Time for some peace and quiet. Really sell them the story about how we had no other choice."

I look across the bedroom, three dead bodies in the corner. Each perfectly rolled up in black bin bags. Laid on top of each other. Headless corpse on the bottom, old geezer in the middle, and My Youngling on top. I turn to my side as Special Enforcer shows himself. He's dressed exactly like the Informers! He's a pseudo-Greco-Roman-Buddhist-monk, Hippie clothing, guns and pecs tensing and pulsing, purple lipstick sparkling, white-heeled shoes, a face mask around his chin, and wearing his white cap with black writing.

"How do I look?"

"You look, err, good…"

"Is that it?"

"I mean, err, well, you look like the Informers. So if that's what you're going for?"

"It is."

"Then you've hit the nail on the head."

"Good."

"Do I look alright in this?"

"Jumper, trousers, and shoes. Yeah, fine."

"You're sure they don't mind?"

"Nah, mate. Specials Enforcers and Informers must follow the company dress code and contractual obligations. Therefore, anything you wear, do, or say falls on me."

"Right. Wow."

"Exactly. What you're wearing is presentable. Try not to do or say anything that looks bad on me, and we should be golden."

"Will do."

"Let's do this then."

"Lead the way, Special Enforcer."

I watch Special Enforcer swagger out of the room like Marylin Monroe down a catwalk. I hear them all light cigarettes and greet each other in unison. As they all laugh and catch up, I inspect the three bagged bodies in the corner of the bedroom. The bodies don't smell as bad as I first thought. I see a dirty toilet brush lying on the bed. It's the one the old geezer shoved up his ass while he was ejaculating over the corpse. I grab a handful of tissues from a box on the bedside table, wrap them around the toilet brush handle and poke the bagged bodies. I tightly grip the shit-covered brush and lightly poke the old geezer in the ribs with my shitty brush. He has matted hair, and his body feels incredibly bony. If I didn't know what was under there, I'd assume it was a greyhound wrapped in a carpet. I move on, poking My Youngling. Compared to the old geezer, he's flabbier. It doesn't feel as though he has any hair. Suddenly, I hear a massive bang from the front room. I drop the brush and run out the door. Special Enforcer and the Informers are all passing around a bottle of rum. They're having a toast and laughing.

"Mr. Sykes!"

"Yeah?"

"Come out of the bedroom and have a drink with us."

"Alright."

I close the door behind me and go over to them. They're all sitting down. I take a seat next to Special Enforcer. He has a swig of rum from the bottle and passes it to me. I hold it to my lips and gulp as much as possible.

"Mr. Sykes! Save some for the Informers."

"Sorry."

I pass the bottle of rum to my nearest Informer. He snatches it from me with his massive hands and downs it like he needs to compete against me. Each Informer takes an enormous gulp in a show of chest-beating masculinity. Mr. Pyjamas has trained them well.

"Let's get to it, shall we?"

Now that everyone has had an excellent drink and a chin wag, Special Enforcer pushes us all to business. We all stay sitting and waiting.

"I'll start, shall I?"

The Informers merely nod as they lean forward in their seats and flex those massive, veiny guns. The veins are tightly stretched like violin strings. They look like I could approach him and start playing Beethoven through his biceps.

"Well, gents, as I said on the phone, it was all in the act of self-defence, wasn't it?"

"Hmm."

I nod in agreement and try to avoid it as much as possible so as not to incriminate me any more than is needed. One of the Informers stands up and holds his hand for Special Enforcer to stop talking. Everybody knows exactly what it means. We all stay silent as Special Enforcer sits back down.

"We want to hear it from Mr. Sykes."

"What?"

"You've told us your side, Special Enforcer."

"I have."

"We want the family man."

My heart starts to beat extremely fast. My legs and hands begin to shake.

"Well?"

"Err, yeah, of course."

I go to speak before the Informer has returned to his seat, but he silences me with his hand and gestures for me to take centre stage in the middle of the circle.

"You want me to…?"

"Tell us your side in the circle's centre, Mr. Sykes."

"Special Enforcer?"

"Go on, mate."

I get a severe case of dry mouth as I stand up and shiver to the circle's centre. Everybody leans forwards in their seats and waits for me to speak. I look around at the gaggle of East Enders in dresses and makeup.

"So, err, basically, yeah, err, as Special Enforcer already mentioned, it was all self-defence. The old geezer had already died, then, err, yeah. The old geezer died while he was getting his end away. Then, err, My Youngling tried to attack us with his, err, his Stanley knife. He was about to slit Special Enforcer's throat to kill him because he'd already killed the old geezer. And, err, we knew what he was capable of. So, err, he had his knife out, err, and we just defended ourselves by slitting his throat with our, I mean, not ours, with, err, with Special Enforcers Stanley knife, yeah."

I stop talking and look around the circle. Special Enforcer plants his head into his hands and looks like he could have a mental breakdown. He rubs the back of his neck very aggressively. The Informers all stare at me like they hate me. One of the other Informers, the one further away from where I was sitting, stands up. He slowly approaches me in the circle. His bloodied heels loudly stomp on the wooden floorboards as red liquid flicks up. The light from the windows shining off his bald bonce. I can just about see his red mush sparkling through his bushy beard. He looks like Jesus walking on water in his white robe. I look at his hands covered in thick, golden coin rings. One punch would knock me out. Or even worse, kill me. The Informer towers over me in his stilettos.

"Which is it?"

My lip starts to quiver, and my throat dries up. I cough loudly to clear my airways.

"Which it what, mate?"

"You had one or two slip ups in retelling the events. Perhaps you misspoke?"

"Mr. Sykes is just nervous, mate. He ain't used to this kind of thing like we are."

Special Enforcer speaks up for me as I stand in the circle's centre, feeling like I could piss myself, dribbling down my tense legs and all over the floor. The Informer would likely slip on my piss. He could fall onto his back, and his robe would come over his head. The Informer's gigantic ten-inch cock and incredibly saggy balls would spread across the floor and drown in rivers of my piss. I'd be forced to hold his cock in my left hand while scrubbing it clean with a cold, damp towel in my right hand. Then I'd be threatened into moving onto his wrinkled ball sack. I'd roll the sack across my knee like I was the Informer's nan knitting him a jumper to keep his bollocks warm in the winter.

"Is that true? Was it just nerves, Mr. Sykes?"

"Yes. It's exactly like Special Enforcer said."

The entire flat is chillingly silent. One Informer stares directly down at me as the other two lean back in their chairs and watch. Special Enforcer can't even look. He just uncomfortably wriggles around and rubs his stubble.

"I understand. You can sit down."

The Informer gestures for me to sit down. I race to my chair. Special Enforcer stares at me with daggers in his eyes. He looks raging. I never thought I'd be that nervous when asked to recount events. The Informer is standing in the centre of the circle. He gestures to his colleagues.

"Can I speak with you in the kitchen?"

All three Informers stand up and walk in unison to the kitchen. They talk amongst themselves. I look over to Special Enforcer.

"You fucking idiot!"

Special Enforcer leaps up from his chair and slaps me around the face.

"Argh! My ears have popped. What the bastard hell was that for? Argh. It feels like you've shattered my ear drum."

I lean to one side to avoid being hit by Special Enforcer. I rub my ear, trying to relieve the swelling.

"You made us both look ridiculous. What was that?"

"I was just nervous, mate. I thought the Informers were going to come at me."

"They probably will now, after that ridiculous performance."

I stay quiet and try to nurse my ear. Special Enforcer looks out of the flat window and repeatedly glances at me. He shakes his head in absolute disgust. I hear the clicking of heels. The Informers make their way from the kitchen. None of them sit down. One of the Informers steps forwards.

"Mr. Sykes."

"Yep."

"Can you come with us, mate?"

"Where?"

"Just into the bedroom."

"Why?"

"We need you to confirm something with the bodies."

"I'll do it instead, gents."

Special Enforcer pipes up, offering to take my place.

"We require the family man to do it."

I stare at Special Enforcer. He looks away from me. I look up at the Informers. All three smile and nod at me. Their red lipstick makes their lips look thick and plump. I'm confident they've all had lip jobs. I stand up and get myself together.

"Yeah, not a problem. Let me lead the way, fellas."

I get some of my confidence back and swagger to the bedroom.

I lead the four of us into the room and close the door behind me. I hear Special Enforcer light a cigarette.

"What do you want me to show you?"

I look at the three Informers, who are all smiling at me.

"It's OK. You can relax."

"What?"

"We don't need you to show us anything."

"Then why are we here?"

"To get you away from Special Enforcer."

"So, there isn't a bedroom body inspection?"

"We've seen and heard all that we need."

"Look, boys, please, I'm fucking sorry. I was just nervous and didn't know what I was saying. Please hear us out again, mate. Listen to Special Enforcer. He can tell you better than I ever could."

"Calm down."

"Please don't hurt me, boys!"

I drop to my knees and burst into tears.

"I'm begging you, lads. I've got Mrs. Sykes and Baby Owl to look after. They need me, don't do this. Me and Mr. Pyjamas agreed that I'd work for his company and be able to send digital currency to support my family. We both signed documents to say he'd leave them alone as long as I worked with him. I only do this job for work. Just ask Mr. Pyjamas. He'll be able to show you the documents. Ask Mr. Pyjamas for the fucking documents!"

"Get off your knees and stop crying."

"Ask Special Enforcer what happened. He's the leader. Ask him!"

"Not anymore."

"What?"

"Special Enforcer isn't your boss anymore. If you get off the floor and wipe your eyes, we can tell you why you're here."

I push myself up from the bedroom floorboards and wipe my tears away. I clean my snotty nose and watery eyes on my jumper. Two Informers are sitting on the bed and flashing me their smooth, shaven, and hairless thighs. They both blow me red kisses of seduction. The other Informer looks down at me with a bright smile.

"Special Enforcer isn't going to be working for us anymore. But you are."

"Err, meaning, err, what exactly?"

"He isn't as committed to the company as you are."

"He is, though! He is!"

"You don't need to defend him so much. He doesn't defend you. Or even like you, if earlier was anything to go by."

"What did he say?"

"He blamed you for everything and asked us to take you in."

"Special Enforcer wouldn't do that. He called me his brother. He wouldn't call me his brother if he didn't love…"

I thought he saw me as his brother? That's what he said. He told me that we were in this together as partners. My head starts to spin, and my stomach ties itself into knots. Are they telling the truth? Did Special Enforcer try to stab me in the back? After everything I've done for him. I was giving him the benefit of the doubt, time after time, after time, after time. Was he attempting to finish the job I'd agreed to sweep to one side? So many questions race around my head.

"He blamed this all on you, Mr. Sykes. We knew from that moment he wasn't a team player. He broke one of the written rules of the company. He was attempting to betray one of his own to save himself. You're a team player. You care about the collective more than yourself. Doing all of this for the benefit of your family. That gains massive points with us."

I can't believe Special Enforcer tried to get one over on me. I'm such a gullible idiot. Any opportunity to have another man take me under his wing. He's not getting away with it.

"What happens next?"

"You'll still be working for Mr. Pyjamas. Whereas Special Enforcer won't."

I wipe away my tears and straighten myself up.

"Who will I be working under now?"

"Nobody. You'll be running things on your own."

"Me?"

"Indeed."

"I don't know how. I'm not a leader, mate. I'm just a follower."

"Not anymore. You run this area's operation for Mr. Pyjamas. After today, you're the boss of this part of the city. We'll teach you and give you everything you need to run things. After that, we'll assign you an assistant. He will be doing the jobs which you and My Youngling did. May he rest in peace."

Destiny is at my door, dragging me into the role I was always meant to play. Finally, after spending a long time as a dirty assistant, I've been given my rightful place. I've earnt this. The details are merely incidental. I'd have become a leader no matter what because that's what the universe had decided from the day I was born. The lion cub becomes the vicious predator.

"Right. Yeah. Thank you."

"As long as you continue to put the collective above yourself, there shouldn't be any issues. Look at Special Enforcer. You don't want that to be you, do you?"

"No. What happens to Special Enforcer?"

"We'll leave now and remove him from your workspace."

"What about the bodies?"

"They're yours to deal with."

"Err…Right..."

"Goes with the job. But you will be getting paid in full. Both Special Enforcer and My Youngling's cut."

I'm going to be paid the total amount. Holy shit!

"Do you accept?"

"I do, my good men, I do."

"That's good to hear."

"Do you all want wanking off?"

"Sorry?"

"Before you leave, do you want me to wank you all off?"

"Why would we ask that of you?"

"Special Enforcer said it was company policy."

"Special Enforcer is a liar."

"I guess morning blowjobs and evening anal aren't company policy either?"

"No, they're not."

The Informers walk out of the room. I close the door and sit on the bed, knowing I'll be paid in full and able to sort out Mrs. Sykes and Baby Owl with enough money to live a healthy and happy life. It makes this all completely worth it. I stare at the dead bodies and listen to Special Enforcer screaming for help as the Informers brutally slash him to pieces.

CHAPTER 9

Six months later, we're on the run.

I slowly slip four fingers underneath the handle. I push upwards and gently massage the inside of the damp, rusty, burnt-out interior. This will do. I roughly pull and struggle. There's no time left to find another car. I've spent over an hour looking, and this one must do. At least this still has its seats and doors all still attached. I open the car door, turn on my phone torch, duck down, and crawl across to the driver's seat, looking behind and using the bright light to check the backseats are safe. I can't find any problems. Other than the fact the car stinks of burning shit and is slowly crumbling apart. Finally, after hours of searching, we have somewhere that we can trust. This car will have to do. If we've been tracked and traced, I can say in our final moments that I tried to find us both somewhere safe to meet. I keep the torch switched on so the entire car shines bright. I keep it on the dashboard in front of me, just above half a steering wheel. God knows what happened to the other half.

It's getting dark outside. Very dark. I hope Bandit can see where I am, and the phone light attracts the tiny bastard. This will be easy to find. It's an old, red, burnt-out car. I've done what I said and found us a secluded spot, so Bandit can stop panicking and having his pathetic midday anxiety attacks. I'm sitting in the driver's seat and feel sharp metal lodging into my back through the wrecked-up seat. I lean forward towards the mirror to stop anything from piercing my spine. The mirror has only got a small crack down the middle. It's probably the least damaged part of the car. While I'm waiting, I try out various things. Flick, click, switch, press, boing. None of it works. Radio, heating, windscreen wipers. All completely fucked-up to pieces.

Where is this fool? I don't care if he's only got little legs that haven't adequately developed or hit puberty yet. He should have been waiting in the carpark early if he's going to use that as an excuse which he often has. I'm leaving if he isn't by my side in twenty minutes. Thirty at the most. I've been on the outskirts of city life for too long now. If Bandit isn't here by the time the full moon is in the sky, I'll return to the warehouse. We'll have to risk our lives by meeting each other there. I probably wouldn't even make it to the warehouse door without being slit, cut, sliced, and chopped to pieces by the Informers. Bandit would risk getting the same treatment. But he isn't the one who has spent months on the outskirts of society to protect and serve our organisation.

I stayed awake all last night and could do with a good wash. I've got cigarette butts in my pockets, black smudges on my hands, and dirt underneath my fingernails. I've been alone, talking to myself for days. My eyelids feel like teabags and my throat is like sandpaper. I can barely stand. I'm shattered. I hear a loud bang coming from behind the car. I snatch my phone from the dashboard, flick the light to full brightness, lean out of the car, and point the light into the darkness. The surrounding environment was utterly destroyed during the ongoing times of troubles. Violent civil wars between all groups.

"Bandit! Oi! Is that you?"

"Yes, boss. Yeah, it's me."

"Well, come and get in the car. I've been waiting a very long time. The passenger door has fallen off. Be careful when you get inside."

I squeeze back into the driving seat and plonk my phone above the steering wheel. My heart and pulse are racing like crazy. I take a couple of deep breaths to stop my hands from shaking. I have my Stanley knife in my jogger's pocket so that I'm ready to fight if one of the Informers happens to find us. Or if one of them has followed Bandit to our meeting. I keep my left hand resting on my pocket and my right hand near the dashboard. Knife and light at the ready.

"Oi! Oi! Saveloy!"

"Fuck's sake, Bandit. You've got to be nice and calm, sunshine. Just like me. Look how chilled and calm I am. Pretty chilled and calm, yeah?"

"I guess so, boss."

"What have I told you about jumping out on me like that?"

"Err, not to do it…"

"And, what have you just done, young man?"

"I did it."

"Never again."

"Sorry, boss."

"It's fine. I apologise for being, y'know, tetchy."

"I understand, boss."

"Under the circumstances, I've got to keep guarded and strong."

"I get it."

"As soon as we move past all of this, I'll calm down."

"I know you will, boss."

"You don't have to keep calling me boss. You're allowed to call me by my name."

"Remind me…?"

"Mr. Sykes is fine."

"Right."

Me and Bandit push back into our car seats. Argh. I can feel the metal digging into my spine. Argh. My poor and precious spine. I grab the half steering wheel and lean forwards.

"Didn't think you'd come."

"Course I was going to come, boss."

"I've been waiting for ages."

"How long?"

"Ten minutes."

"Ten minutes isn't that long, boss."

"It's quite long."

"Not as long as six months."

"Oi!"

I slap Bandit around the back of his head, knocking him forward until his face nearly smashes against the dashboard. His nose cracks on the side, and he falls back into his seat. He pinches his nose. I could have broken his snout. An awkward silence fills the car. I don't think he's bleeding. It serves him right to be so disrespectful to an elder.

"Bandit…"

"Yeah?"

"I'm sorry."

"It's alright, boss."

"Mr. Pyjamas doesn't want to stab you to death, does he? It's me that he's after."

"I guess so…"

"Otherwise, he would have had the Informers drag you in by now."

"Yeah."

"You look different, young man. Have you done something different to your hair?"

"No, boss,"

"Lost weight?"

"Maybe a tiny bit."

"Thought so."

"All of the stress, boss."

"How do you think I feel?"

"I know, I know."

We both take deep breaths and blow air out of the windows. The only thing keeping us from complete darkness is the light on my phone. Some more awkward silence fills the car. There's a nice breeze against my face. Earlier in the day, there was a clear, blue sky. I used to hate that kind of weather. A summertime blue with a winter chill. But now I love it. It makes me feel alive and excited for sunrise.

"Let's just get down to the facts, Bandit."

"Sure."

"Did anybody follow you here?"

"No."

"Positive?"

"Yep."

"Are they still watching the warehouse?"

"Yep."

"Fuck!"

"But not twenty-four-seven."

"What?"

"The Informers are waiting for you to return, so they don't always watch the warehouse."

"How long?"

"What?"

"How long do they spend watching the warehouse?"

"Twelve hours."

"Twelve hours maximum?"

"Yep."

"That's great. You've just got to track when they leave, and I can come back."

I hear a light drizzle hitting the front window. I lean out of the car door and feel droplets of rain on my head. Earlier, just one grey cloud seemed to be turning black. The sky remained blue and seemed at war with the black cloud. I always trust that the summertime sky will win against the evil blackness in the end. Even this drizzle will be defeated. I pull back into the car and look at a nervous, Bandit.

"There's one issue."

"What?"

"The Informers trashed the warehouse."

"Trashed it?"

"Yep."

"Like what?"

"They've ripped everything apart, tore it down, burnt most of it, funnily enough. The bits they couldn't demolish, they removed by force. So everything's either wrecked or been taken. There's nothing left."

"There's nothing left in there to work with?"

"No, not really. Every time I've snuck into the gaff, it didn't seem like we could ever work out of there again."

"What about Mrs. Sykes and Baby Owl?"

"They're great, boss."

"How?"

"They're still living off the money you've sent them. From what I could see, they both looked in good health."

"Has any of Mr. Pyjamas' Informers come looking for them?"

"Nah."

"Are you sure?"

"One hundred percent."

"How do you know?"

"I've got mates who also live in the villages. I'm not sure why, but Mr. Pyjamas has stuck to his side of the agreement. He can't send his Informers into the villages, and nobody from the villages can go into the cities."

"But are your mates also on the run from the company?"

"Some of them, yeah. But Mr. Pyjamas is expanding his businesses. He still relies on the villages for trade and work. It doesn't serve him well to start an all-out civil war."

"What will happen if the Informers look for Mrs. Sykes and Baby Owl? It starts a war between land and city?"

"Yeah, boss."

"The Informers are sticking to their end of things too?"

"You don't need to worry, boss. Stop panicking. I've been to the villages multiple times. Your wife and kid are glowing and have plenty to live off."

"That's amazing. Thanks, Bandit. Very much appreciated."

"The villages are incredible. Highly religious. Nature. Family. Tradition."

"That's fantastic, Bandit."

"The warehouse is more an issue."

"Right…"

"Not only are the Informers on the lookout for you, boss, but the city is an absolute mess. Looting and violence between identity groups, pretty much all of the time. When they aren't fighting, they're fucking. Especially in the city centre right near the warehouse. Most buildings are burnt down. At night time, a lot of places are being used for sex parties and orgies. Illegal surgeries, abortions, drug overdoses, and murders. The list goes on, boss."

I crouch and squeeze my way out of the smelly rusty craphole. I leave the light shining to see what's outside and directly in front of me.

I begin to walk around the car in circles. Back and forth with my hands on my head. Bandit pushes himself out of the car and does the same. We walk around the car with our hands on our heads. I look up at the night sky, which looks beautiful. The full moon is here to stay. The full moon is here to play.

"The drizzle has stopped, Bandit."

"What drizzle, boss?"

"It doesn't matter…"

Unlike everything else, the ongoing troubles will never affect the gorgeous full moon. Nobody can riot or get an abortion on the moon.

"What now, boss?"

"I've been sleeping in a small shack about a mile away, deep in the woods, surrounded by trees. If you think it's dark now, you want to see the state of my shack at night. It will take me hours to find my way there. Let's hope my phone doesn't die. I'll be sleeping in this car if I don't have the light to get back. No one will find me in my shack. I'll devise a plan for us both."

"A plan for what?"

"If they want a war, I'll give them a fucking war."

"Are we done playing nice, boss?"

"Just call me Mr. Sykes!"

"Sorry, it's a bad habit."

"We're done playing nice. We haven't spent six months, the two of us, setting up a rival company against Mr. Pyjamas, to be driven out of our gaff and having to hide away. My daughter will soon be eighteen months old. I've not seen her in person since two days after her birth. She won't have a clue who I am. I've spoken to Mrs. Sykes and regularly wired over digital currency. Still, I know she hates me for getting us into this and will never take me back. So the war against Mr. Pyjamas is on. I don't know how yet, but we'll get there. We're taking it back to the Informers."

"Have you heard about The Hunt?"

"What's The Hunt?"

"It's a new off-shoot company that Mr. Pyjamas set up. He's created like a, err, what are they called? New paid, err, a trained army! A private army. That's the one. Yeah, yeah, yeah. He's setting up a private army to remove their enemies. The army is called The Hunt. They have all of the latest, y'know, technological stuff. They're fully equipped. Mr. Pyjamas has gone to town supplying The Hunt with its weapons. They're ready to go. They're moving on from the slitting and slashing. That's old school, baby tactics of violence. Mr. Pyjamas and his Informers are trying to be more sophisticated now."

"Why are they doing this, Bandit?"

"Their empire has expanded, and rival companies are popping up everywhere, especially with the civil wars. Most people only have household weapons. Knives and bats. But some of the gadgets The Hunt can work with. Wow!"

"Like what?"

"Robotic guns and grenades. Shit like that."

"What do they do?"

"I'm not sure. But it works."

"Why are you bringing it up if you don't know?"

"Mr. Pyjamas has paid The Hunt for your head."

"My head?"

"The word is out for you. All across the internet and rumours throughout the city. The paid warrant is massive, boss."

I slowly walk away from Bandit. I'm shaking. I'm unsure if that's because it's cold outside or if my anxiety is kicking off. Probably a bit of both. I bend down and get back into the craphole car. I look at my phone, and the battery is racing to zero. If I want to sleep in the shack tonight, I'll need the battery for the light. Otherwise, it's this iceberg shit sandwich. Bandit crawls back into his doorless passenger seat.

"Bandit?"

"Yes, Mr. Sykes."

I smile at Bandit to show my appreciation for his respect.

"Our business isn't big enough. Just the two of us."

"How do we recruit more members?"

"We travel around the villages on the city outskirts."

"How do we do that?"

"Walk."

"Right."

"The outskirt villages are full of people who hate the Informers. People who, like us, are on the run from Mr. Pyjamas. People who have been banished from the cities with threats of violence or murder. People who once worked with the Informers were told to leave. Tons and tons have run out of the city for a life away from those companies. Alone and scared. Sometimes families need protection. We can leave all this behind and recruit the villages to help us. Join our barbarian warband. Could they help us expand the business? Make ourselves rich! Special Enforcer always joked about turning on Mr. Pyjamas to start a rival business. But instead, the Judas turned on me."

"Where do you think Special Enforcer is now?"

"Burning in Hell."

"You believe in Hell?"

"I sure do."

"Err, then, why…"

"Why have I done so much to hurt people if I believe in Hell?"

"Yes, sir…"

"I'm willing to make the eternal sacrifice for my family. My soul in Hell for Mrs. Sykes' and Baby Owl's soul on Earth."

"When shall we leave, boss?"

"Tonight."

"I can't do tonight."

I raise my hand and clip Bandit in the jaw, making him fall out of the car and to the concrete. He rolls over to hold his jaw and lies on his back. He doesn't speak or make a sound. I lean over to the passenger seat and stare out at Bandit.

"You'll do whatever I tell you, yeah?"

Bandit doesn't speak. He lies on the cold, damp, hard ground. I may have knocked him out. Bandit looks up at the night sky and begins to cry. The feeling of guilt completely overtakes me. I hate myself for hitting Bandit. The stress is too much to handle. I can't help but take it out on the person closest to me, even if it does make me hate myself afterward.

"Hmm."

"You good?"

"Hmm."

"I'm sorry, Bandit."

"It's fine, Mr. Sykes."

I go outside to check on Bandit. First, I walk around the car to him. Then, I bend over and gently lift him to his feet.

"Why can't you leave tonight?"

"All of my equipment is still in the den."

"Right."

"Yep."

"I thought you'd moved it?"

"That was only if the Informers got a whiff of the den."

"They didn't?"

"Nah, boss."

"Right."

"They've been so obsessed with the warehouse that I never got tracked to the den."

"Why don't you collect it all tonight, and we meet here early tomorrow morning."

"How early?"

"Sunrise."

"Err…"

"What?"

"That's early, boss."

"Well, I wanted to go tonight."

"Right, yeah, err, you're right."

"Thank you, Bandit. How very kind of you. I'll do my bit."

"What's your bit, Mr. Sykes?"

"My phone's going to die any minute now. I'll sleep in the smelly, burnt, ice-cold, shit sandwich car without a single speck of light. I probably won't sleep. I'll stay awake for hours and hours. Making our plan for tomorrow morning. Alone and waiting for sunrise to come."

"Wow. That's amazing, boss."

"The least you can do is play your part in all this. Bring everything we might need. Pack a bag with as many essentials as possible, especially different phones and chargers. You won't be able to get hold of me when mine dies. You've got to be here as early as possible."

"I will, boss."

"Make sure you don't get followed."

"I promise."

"Good lad."

I kiss Bandit on the cheek.

"See you in the morning, boss. I mean Mr. Sykes!"

"Run along, kiddo."

Bandit sprints across what looks like an abandoned toxic wasteland. Before I know it, he's disappeared into the woodland area. It's not too far from the city if he keeps running at that speed. Hopefully, he follows my orders and we can move forward. Both come out of hiding and take on Mr. Pyjamas. No more running away and being terrified.

My phone dies, and the light completely disappears. I'm alone in the pitch-black car park. I feel blind. There's more brightness when I close my eyes than outside. I'm wearing a pair of white trainers, so I can just about make my way around the car and back into the driver's seat. I triple-check my phone, and its battery has wholly gone. It would be hopeless trying to get back to the woodland shack. I close my eyes and tightly grip my Stanley knife. As I hear the wind howling, I pull my hood over my head and try to curl up into a ball. I begin to map out a plan in my head. I try to work out how we can move forward with my terrible idea. Upon further inspection of recruiting people out of town to form some rebel war group, it seems ridiculous. I realise I have absolutely no idea what I'm talking about.

CHAPTER 10

Me and Bandit are both dressed in our usual grey joggers, black hoodies, and white trainers. There are stains and marks all over our clothes. Bandit wears a black cap, whereas I just let my hair do what it wants. My scruffy, uncut beard hides my dirty face and makes me look ten years older. I look like I've lived in a cave high up in the mystical mountains. Bandit uses his cap to cover his disgusting, childish chops. Bandit washes whenever he goes back to his den.

In comparison, I haven't had a proper wash in months. My shack doesn't have a sink. I use whatever Bandit brings when we meet in the woodland area halfway from my hut. I'll tip water bottles over my head and let it drip down my body. Bandit is young and fast, so he can usually go into a broken shop, quickly grab something, and run away before anybody gets to him. That's why he's my right-hand man, selected and chosen to help me through these challenging times. I'd be nothing without him. I would be dead. Bandit is the son I never had. Although I've never told him or let on that's how I feel.

Bandit has a rucksack of food, drinks, and weapons packed for our journey to the outskirts of villages. We're currently in the city's centre, surrounded by the previous night's riots and gang violence. Most of it was funded and promoted by Mr. Pyjamas. His businesses and fighters are some of the most financially stable and well put together. But I know Mr. Pyjamas inside out. I know how to end him. I know how to bring his whole organization crashing down into obscurity.

Most importantly, I know how to end his life. A golden bullet straight between the eyes. Just like everybody else. Mr. Pyjamas has doubled down on the control of his famous golden bullets. He only allows his most trusted associates anywhere near them instead of handing them out like sweets. The days of letting customers and workers use them for personal gain are long gone. He's terrified and aware that the slightest slip up could end him.

I've spent enough time with Mr. Pyjamas to know his weak spots. He's always assured me that a golden bullet takes care of everything. The first time I shot a bullet, I saw its magnificence glow as the sunlight blazed through the double-glazed windows of my great aunt's house. I could genuinely hear soft, classical music playing in my head as the foretold brilliance of the pistol was evident.

I remember grabbing the pistol and pointing it in Ravemachines face. He knew that I had gotten the better of him. The pistol was a lot heavier than I imagined. It weighed my arm towards the floor. I quickly pulled my arm up, straightened it, and aimed for Ravemachines head. Then, I firmly clicked the trigger.

The golden bullet sprang out of the pistol; the rest is history. That historic moment plays in my mind daily. Before I left the business, I managed to keep hold of one of my unique, shining silver saviours. I sent it to Mrs. Sykes for her protection.

Me and Bandit smell like vulgar, scruffy raggers. So much so that we picked up a bloke on our way through the city. He's travelling with us to the villages, as he allegedly has family there that he needs to see. His name is Tagger. He knows a quicker way through the city and around the riots. A path that will take half the time and cause us half the trouble. He's a middle-aged tramp with a viscous rottweiler dog named Britain. Tagger has warned us how violent Britain can be. He told us not to stare at him or make any sudden movements.

We have a rough and tough rottweiler to help if anybody messes with us. But at the same time, Tagger has said if he locks his jaw, he'll be able to rip our fingers off our hands. The only way to release Britain's locked jaw would be to stick our fingers up its asshole! Start fingering Britain's hole until he lets go. Suppose we encounter Mr. Pyjamas' Informers or The Hunt. In that case, Tagger assures us that the rottweiler would be the first to lock his jaw on their faces and ultimately tear them to pieces. We've got vicious Britain, and they'll have to finger a dog's asshole to stop their hand from being ripped off.

Tagger and Britain have lived on the streets for years, eating out of bins, nibbling on food scrapings off the uncleaned concrete, and drinking from mucky puddles after it rains. Tagger and Britain are both addicted to cri-cringle-brekk, a new street drug invented by one of the city gangs. It's a pill that you crush up, sniff, and lick. If you buy a couple of capsules of cri-cringle-brekk, you can crush them into a mountainous pile and trip your balls off. It's equivalent to smack and crack in strength. You don't need all the needles, pipes, and spoons like you do when you're a smackhead or crackhead. Cri-cringle-brekk is so strong that you can only take small amounts. Me and the other three scruffy raggers drag ourselves through the disgusting city centre. It's chillingly silently and worryingly empty. Not a soul in sight. Not a sound in the air. A ghost town. This lazy, incompetent, degenerate society will still fall asleep as the sun rises. Sexual orgies, drug parties, slashings and slittings, and dodgy dealings occur when the sun goes down. When the sun is up, we're forced to look at the horrific mess the decadents left behind. The Informers roam the streets to gain and sustain as much power, money, and territory as possible.

"Bandit?"

"Yes, boss."

"We're coming up to the warehouse."

"Yeah."

"Won't people be waiting outside?"

"For what?"

"For me."

"Oh, err…"

"You were the one who said that some Informers spent half their time waiting at the warehouse for me."

"Ah, so I did."

"You told me that a high price was put on my head?"

"It is, boss."

"So…"

"So, err, what, boss?"

"Shouldn't you check if they're outside waiting for me?"

"Oh, shit! Yeah, that makes sense, Mr. Sykes."

"We'll wait for you here, Bandit."

Bandit quickly sprints ahead. He uses his young, healthy, flexible limbs to jump over any torn-apart and broken obstacles that stand in his way. Me and Tagger wait by an old café burnt to the ground. We look on through the blackened streets with Britain by our side.

"Sorry about him, Tagger. He's still very young."

"It's alright, mate. We were all his age once."

"Exactly."

"He seems like a reliable lad?"

"Yeah, mate. He sure is."

"He's not your family?"

"Nah. Well, err, y'know, not technically speaking."

"Like a son to you?"

"Yeah, yeah he is."

"I know the feeling."

"He's the nearest thing I've got to family."

"That's the same with me and Britain."

"Hmm."

"Wife and kids all fucked off to the villages. Left me on the city streets. Alone, homeless, starving, dehydrated, addicted…"

"Must have been hard?"

"It was until Britain came along."

"How did you two meet?"

"She belonged to my dealer."

"Right."

"I went to his flat to buy a couple of capsules. I'd not had a fix, slept, or eaten in days. I'd got some digital currency together on one of those currency cards. Y'know the ones?"

"I know the ones."

"The ones you put currency onto and can send to digital devices."

"My wife uses them all of the time."

"I went to the dealer's flat with one of the cards and sent him currency for some cri-cringle-brekk. We did the deal. He let me crush the pills on his table. I went to sniff, but he grabbed me and screamed, 'Lick don't sniff!' I thanked him for the reminder. I licked the cri-cringle-brekk off his table and started tripping balls. Next thing I know, he points a shotgun in my face and thinks it's funny to pretend he will blow my head off. I freak out and try to stand up. But I can't. My legs were gone. They had run away from my body. The dealer laughs his head off. This is when Britain runs into the room. Britain tries to defend me from the dealer's vicious threats. In return, the dealer kicked the fuck out of Britain. He was lying in the middle of the room. He couldn't move. Once I'd stopped tripping so hard and got the feeling back in my legs, I waited until the dealer went to the bathroom, picked up Britain, and left. I never used that dealer or saw him again. We got to know each other for a couple of weeks. Living on the streets together. I never checked in on my old wife and kids."

"But now you are?"

"Exactly. Now we are."

I have no idea what to say. Me and Tagger look in opposite directions. Bandit comes sprinting back towards us. He's gasping for air and trying to catch his breath.

"It's alright, just relax, Bandit."

Once Bandit finally calms down and gets his breath back, he relays the news.

"Nobody's there, Mr. Sykes."

"There were no Informers or gangs or anybody?"

"Not a soul, boss. I didn't see anybody the whole way."

"Well, if everything's clear, then lead the way, Bandit."

"Sure thing, Mr. Sykes."

Bandit walks beside us and leads us in the right direction. The four of us make our way toward the warehouse. According to Tagger, we go through that part of the city, leading to a shortcut toward the village. This shortcut will shorten our journey by half the time. We should be on the boarders within an hour instead of two. We stumble through the fallen ghost town, not a soul in sight.

We arrive at our old, abandoned warehouse. I stare at the four-storey building missing every window, the broken glass scattered all over the road. The roof tiles have come crashing down and broken into pieces along the pavement. The black metal door dumped in the doorway. I look around the rooftops of the building to see if we're being watched. It stinks of vinegar. But not the flavouring that can be poured onto your fish and chips, but the type of vinegary stench that comes from a guy's unwashed testicles.

"Shall I lead the way from here, lad?"

"Go for it, Tagger."

Tagger points us in his direction with Britain by his side, as me and Bandit follow him toward the villages.

Tagger takes us through streets and back alleys, which I didn't know existed. We're forced to see the dead bodies and decapitated animals. Babies and young children are chopped into pieces. Tagger knew where he was taking us but never warned us of the horrific barbarity we would see. Finally, after walking for roughly one hour through what looked like the aftermath of a bloodied terrorist attack or high tide flood, we arrived at the border.

Tagger and Britain lead the way up a steep hill of greenery. There had been wooden steps to climb, but they were torn to pieces, so we had to use all of our leg strength to push our way up the mountainous hill. Halfway up, I see Tagger, Britain, and Bandit. I'm the last one to reach the top.

The view is beautiful. It takes my breath away. The four of us stare ahead at the clear blue skies, perfect green grass, and excellent quaint cottages in the distance. I look back and see the horrible and disgusting city we had left behind. I keep telling myself that the only reason I've lived and worked in that shit hole is that Mrs. Sykes and Baby Owl could live in the heavenly villages. We are silent on the high hill, all thinking about what this journey means to us individually. We look at each other, all wondering the same thing. How the hell do we get over this huge twenty-foot fence? I've not got a fucking clue. I didn't know a huge, caged fence separated the village and city. We all glare at the top of the hill with our heads up and shoulders back. We are staring at the metal fence keeping apart the two communities.

"Why didn't you tell me there was a fence, Bandit?"

"There isn't on the other side, boss."

"Is it electrified?"

"I think so, boss."

"Shit."

"I don't remember this fence been here either, lads."

As the scorching sun rains on our sweaty bodies, the four of us crash onto the grass. Britain is snoring on Tagger's lap. Tagger sits with his legs crossed and jaw scraping across the dirt. Bandit is bright red as he sweats and gasps for a fresh breeze. If I'm being honest, I will let anything happen to me to keep the family safe. This includes Bandit. I slowly push myself up from the grass, brush the crap off my hands, roll up my sleeves, and think of a way to get us over this fence.

CHAPTER 11

We walk through the village with a spring in our step. I'm amazed that such beauty can exist in a world where pure decadence and degeneracy have rotted the insides of a species. Nevertheless, the villages have managed to set up local shops and cafes. Gorgeous cottages and public gardens. Friends drinking coffee on small tables outside, like in twentieth-century Paris! I can see Joyce and Beckett smoking pipes and scoffing pastries. Families are eating homegrown, organic breakfasts and freshly squeezed orange juice. Gothic cathedrals are shaking hands with God. Picnics in the park as a first date. Small pubs of local beer and working men of the modern era. The fresh air which hasn't been over-polluted and the incredible smell of flowers. Every human sense is romantically lured in by a place that has been allowed to return to man's most authentic nature. An excellent walk through the village, speaking to young, fit, healthy strangers. I am waved to by the elderly, so full of wisdom, smiled at by the young children, so full of youth. I don't think I've ever seen the delights: religion, family, and spirit.

I can see why Mr. Pyjamas and the Informers agreed not to touch the villages. It's clear why he's allowed them to live in peace for so long. They agreed to trade most of their hard-earned labour and products. The villages do all of the work. Mr. Pyjamas pays them for their services. The two leave each other alone.

But it's confirmed the direction which Mr. Pyjamas is taking. He plans to use his trained private armies and personal securities. I'm sure it's only a matter of time before he starts the foreseen invasion. He's turning back on his agreed deal and taking everything from the villagers by force and violence. He wants them to work as his slaves who will lose their lives if they step out of line.

Mr. Pyjamas' plan is to combine both city and village. To turn these fantastic lands into the disgraceful society he turned the once flourishing city into.

But not on my watch.

As long as I have a family who lives here, I'll do everything I can to protect them. The villagers look so comfortable, relaxed, and at peace that they wouldn't be willing to listen to a scoundrel such as me. They wouldn't believe an invasion was coming if I screamed it from the town square. The village community is far too at peace to be able to defend themselves or even allow themselves to feel negative emotions towards the other.

We arrive at Mrs. Sykes' cottage. I give four light knocks on the wooden door, and we wait for Mrs. Sykes to let us in. I'm terrified. Nobody answers. I look to my left toward Bandit, who still has a thick purple lip from where I punched him. To my right sits Britain, our new rottweiler dog. Where's Tagger? Let's say he never made it over the fence. It turns out the colossal fence wasn't electrified after all. Tagger fell backward off the top and smashed his head on the solid concert. Me and Bandit could have helped him. But we didn't. We watched as he choked to death on his blood and vomit. We assumed Britain would attack us since he was allegedly so in love and dedicated to Tagger. But he didn't. Instead, Britain licked Tagger's blood off our hands. He softly rubbed himself against our legs, rolled on his back so we could rub his belly, finally scratched Tagger's eyes with his sharp claws, and viciously tore his face apart with savage teeth. Nobody stuck a finger up Britain's asshole to stop him.

"Doesn't sound like she's home, boss."

"I'm trying to listen, Bandit."

I can hear the faint sound of classical music playing from the cottage. I press my ear to the door and hear Mozart's Piano Sonata No. 11. I remember the old geezer who died under my and Special Enforcer's services telling me this was his favourite song of Mozart's.

"Can you hear that, Bandit?"

"Yeah, I can hear it."

Listen closer. Bandit presses his ear against the door. Britain comes between my legs and pushes his rottweiler ears against the door to hear the music.

"Who's playing, Mr. Sykes?"

"That's Mozart, Bandit."

"Who?"

"The greatest musical composer of all time."

"What's a musical composer?"

"Nothing."

"But it's a good thing?"

"Amazing."

"Wow."

"Yep."

"Who do you think is listening?"

"I think Mrs. Sykes is listening."

"Why isn't she answering the door, boss?"

"I don't know, mate."

I pull away from the door and consider the possibilities as to why the three of us have been standing here like a gang of idiots. Bandit thuds on the door several times. Still no answer. Either Mrs. Sykes is intentionally ignoring us, or there's been some accident. Maybe she's fallen or been killed?

"Keep knocking until she answers, Mr. Sykes. We'll walk up and down the street and look at the beautiful cottages."

"That sounds like a good idea, Bandit."

A couple of hours later.

I'm sitting at Mrs. Sykes' old-fashioned kitchen table. The kitchen's floral décor and multi-coloured table mats make me feel like I'm in an episode of one of the old daytime television soaps. It's definitely a step down from our old house. Then again, who am I to talk? She hasn't done much to keep the new cottage in a charming condition. There's an overbearing smell of damp clothes. I look over my shoulder and see a pile of socks and pants lying on the windowsill. I lean over and touch her lacy black underwear. I skim my fingers over the large stack of socks. They're soaking wet. Mrs. Sykes has done a wash and not bothered to dry them. Even the flowery kitchen tiles are covered in black stains. The colourful cupboards need new handles, and the hard floor has cracks. When I walked through the hall, shoes were scattered across the floor.

The garden of the cottage is the complete opposite. It looks even better than our old garden at the great aunt's house. The sounds of birds chirping in the trees. As though they're having a conversation with each other. The birds never interrupt. They wait for one to stop tweeting and then respond politely. Everything is so fresh and meaningful. Nature has been preserved and is something that Mrs. Sykes looks after.

Mrs. Sykes sits opposite and hands me a glass of water.

"Cheers."

I pick up the glass and down the water in one go.

"Thirsty?"

"Yeah."

"Want another?"

"I'm good, cheers."

"Let me know when you do."

"Will do."

"Right."

"Nice place."

"Thank you.

"Very quaint."

"Your money is well spent."

"This is the first time I've seen it."

"I know…"

"Interesting to see what I'm paying for."

"Hmm."

"Well, err, I'm just doing what we agreed."

"Baby Owl loves it."

"That's all that matters."

"Yep."

"Where is Baby Owl?"

"Ah, she's at her friend's house."

"She's got friends, already?"

"Yep."

"At eighteen months?"

"Yep."

"Right."

"So, what are you doing here?"

My throat begins to dry out. I need that second glass of water, after all. I begin to cough.

"Are you alright?"

"Hmm."

"More water?"

"Hmm."

I stop coughing as Mrs. Sykes fills my glass with fresh water and puts the glass down next to me. I drink the water down in one. Mrs. Sykes sits opposite me. We resume.

"Sorry, Mrs. Sykes, err, the thing is, sorry, it's just we haven't spoken for such a long time. It's hard to know where to start."

"It's OK. Just take your time."

Mrs. Sykes' gentleness relieves me of my nerves. My dry throat disappears, and I needn't rely on water to get me through.

"I've not spoken to you in a long time."

"I know."

"I thought I'd come to see you."

"It's good to see you."

"But, err, there is another reason I had to leave the city. I'm not working for Mr. Pyjamas anymore."

"I've heard the rumours."

"Rumours?"

"Everybody's heard. The reward for your head is quite a big one."

"I'm fine, though."

"I never had any doubt that you wouldn't be. You're the strongest man I've ever known."

I could cry. But I don't. Mrs. Sykes grabs my hand and rubs my knuckles with her soft thumbs. Me and Mrs. Sykes look into each other's eyes. I get a queasy sensation in the pit of my stomach and feel like screaming at the top of my voice. Wow. She's amazing. So fucking beautiful. Wow. I feel nervous that I'm reading too much into this. What if she's got a boyfriend that I don't know about? We both turn away and look into the gorgeous garden.

It feels like we still have such a connection. This may be destiny. The planets, stars, and spiritual dimensions have aligned so that we would meet. God may have manipulated the physical realm so that me and Mrs. Sykes could become one again.

A mixture of the green and natural beauty of Mrs. Sykes overtakes my heart and spirit. It gives me a sense of awe and confidence. We lock lips and share a long, soft kiss that lasts a few minutes before pulling away with huge grins. We look outside at the blue sky and hold hands across the table. I don't have a care in the world. I can only feel the excitement and a deep sense of gratitude. I imagine getting down onto my hands and knees, praying to God, and thanking him for this experience. Is God pure love? I thought my life was over, and I no longer had a purpose except as a workhorse for other people. But I suddenly have hope for the future. It feels like a depressing epoch is ending so that a new and better one can begin.

Mrs. Sykes smiles widely and shows me her sparkling white teeth. We kiss again. This kiss is passionate but sloppy at the same time. It almost feels like the kind of kiss you would have in secondary school. Lots of tongue and salvia.

Me and Mrs. Sykes crash our way into her front room. We continue our passionate, sloppy kissing as Mrs. Sykes kicks off her shoes, and I kick off my trainers. She shoves me backwards onto her sofa and dives onto my lap. I kiss Mrs. Sykes' neck as she pulls her top over her head and throws it to the floor. She's on top of me in her black bra. We continue to kiss before standing up. I rip off my T-shirt, and we pull down our trousers. We stare at each other's bodies. Mrs. Sykes is in better shape than me. She's standing in her lacy black bra and knickers and has this incredibly toned body. I'm in my damp, dirty boxers and tense up to look like I have a bit of muscle. Mrs. Sykes leads the way, removing her black bra, showing her big round boobs and perfect light brown nipples. Mrs. Sykes grabs my hands and pushes them onto her chest. My dick gets incredibly hard! So much so that it feels like it will blast off my body. I rub her nipples between my fingers as she gently moans and gawps at my bulge, nearly ripping out of my boxers.

Mrs. Sykes burst out laughing. I feel slightly embarrassed. Does she think my tit-juggling technique is terrible? I'll be happy to learn how to massage breasts correctly! Mrs. Sykes pulls down her black knickers and encourages me to remove my boxers. We return to our passionate kissing as she pushes me backward onto the sofa. Before I know it, she's grabbing my dick and pushing inside her. It's so wet and tight that I'm confident I'll blow. I clench my ass cheeks so I don't explode so quickly. She encourages me to go faster and harder as she moans louder. It doesn't take me long to shoot my load inside Mrs. Sykes. As I go to pull out of her, she holds me and keeps my dick inside. As she strokes my hair, I rest my head on her perfectly round boobs. Mrs. Sykes gently rubs my head. Neither of us says a word. Both are still gasping and trying to get our breath back. This is just like old times. Better, in fact. The best sex we've had in years.

"I love you."

"I love you too, Mr. Sykes."

An hour later, me and Mrs. Sykes sit back at the table.

"When's Mr. Pyjamas going to invade?"

"Next couple of days."

"Get us out of here, Mr. Sykes."

"I promise that I will. Then, when you're both safe, I will kill him. Do you still have those golden bullets I sent you?"

"I'll go get them."

Mrs. Sykes jumps up from the table and runs through the door. I hear her sprint upstairs and open what sounds like cupboard doors. I hear Mrs. Sykes scurrying about and opening various boxes, looking for my golden bullets. Suddenly, there's a thunderous banging on the front door. It gets louder. Mrs. Sykes is still upstairs. I leave the table and walk through the hall. I open the door. It's Bandit and Britain. They're both frantically bouncing around like a pair of poorly animated cartoon characters.

"What do you want?"

"Mr. Sykes!"

"I'm in the middle of something, Bandit."

"They're here, boss."

"Who's here?"

"Mr. Pyjamas! And, the, err, The Hunt, and they've ripped down the entire fence!"

"Whereabouts are they?"

"They're making their way down the roads toward the centre. About five minutes away from the Cathedral."

"Ah, Jesus Christ!"

"What do we do, Mr. Sykes?"

"Have they started shooting or anything?"

"Not that I know of."

"Both of you come inside."

Bandit and Britain run past me as I slam the door closed. The three of us quickly hurry into the kitchen. Mrs. Sykes gallops downstairs.

"What's happening? I heard all the shouting and looked out of the bedroom window. Big groups dressed in black are marching towards the village centre."

"Everybody sit down and listen to me."

"Boss?"

"I said fucking sit, Bandit!"

Bandit, Britain, and Mrs. Sykes all take a seat. I walk around the kitchen in circles and try to get my thoughts together.

"You three stay here. Keep the doors locked, and don't leave the house. Make sure Baby Owl doesn't leave her friend's house. Call her friend's parents, Mrs. Sykes. She's not to fucking leave, you hear me?"

"Yeah."

I grab the shining silver saviour and golden bullets from the table. Mrs. Sykes, Bandit, and Britain ramble and mumble amongst themselves. I ignore them and head towards the door.

"I love you, Mr. Sykes."

Mrs. Sykes gives me a passionate kiss.

"I love you, too."

I head for the door with my pistol in hand.

"Mr. Sykes?"

"Yes, Bandit?"

"Give him a golden bullet from me."

"I will do, son."

Britain scurries over and barks. He softly rubs himself against my knee before plodding back to Bandit.

"Thanks, Britain. You too, mate."

I head out the door, and Mrs. Sykes closes and locks it behind me. I hear loud screams and gunshots not too far away. I hobble on my injured ankle toward the bullets and explosions.

CHAPTER 12

I'm crouched under the seats in one of the enormous Gothic churches.

I have a loaded, shining silver saviour in one hand, packages of the golden bullets in my coat pocket, and my other hand pushing down onto the concrete floor. Mr. Pyjamas and his private army have demolished the entire village. It's only taken them a couple of hours to force their way through and destroy nearly everything.

They're not killing any of its citizens, only obliterating and tearing down the astonishing architecture and marvellous small businesses. Most buildings, with a few exceptions, such as the Churches, lie in ruins. Like the fall of Rome. Or the collapse of Constantinople. It's to be duly noted that Mr. Pyjamas has ordered and demanded, over and over again, that The Hunt is to use their weapons to destroy the material parts of the villages. Not a human being is to be intentionally killed. Somehow those caught in an accident or blown to pieces while still in a building don't count! Mr. Pyjamas' intentions are apparent. As I first suspected. He wants to combine the city and villages into one giant state he can rule. To buy up every corporation and business. At the same time, leaving all the heavy lifting and hard graft to the ordinary working man. The Hunt has even decimated nature, tearing apart the trees and greenery. Shot the wildlife and ripped up the parks. The villages will soon look like the city, demolished beauty overtaken by psychopathic power dynamics.

I've been hiding for quite some time, spying on Mr. Pyjamas and watching his every move, having to be extra careful not to get caught. He's got more than enough workforce to take me out in seconds.

I hear the Church doors crash open and smash against the solid walls. The Hunt enters one by one. Black boots are stomping against the concrete floor. I tightly grip my pistol and press my body against the floor, keeping myself up with my other hand. The Hunt stomp about the Church while I silently watch. They're looking tired. Maybe even lazy. They are holding their rifles beside them with such a loose grip that it wouldn't take much for their tried fingers to slip, dropping them to the ground. They're certainly not holding them like they still have a job to do. Even their black boots start to scrape against the concrete like a sleepy child, as opposed to strong and muscular legs which are ready to fight.

I slowly and quietly push my head toward a peephole through the chairs. There's enough wood to cover my head and plenty of room to move freely. I look out at The Hunt. There aren't as many soldiers as I thought. There are only three inside the Church. They all sit down and rest their rifles on the ground.

This is my perfect opportunity to act.

I crawl backward underneath the seats, double check the shining silver saviour is loaded, push myself upward, lean over the chairs, and whip out my pistol. All three of The Hunt jump to their feet. Their jaws scrape across the floor as they scurry about like wasps. They've clearly never been trained for such an event. Each one of them has an issue. Solider one drops his rifle onto the floor. Solider two slips and falls back into his seat. Solider three runs and tries to escape, also dropping his rifle on the way.

I straighten my right arm.

WOOSH!

BANG!

The golden bullet hits soldier one right between the eyes. His head splatters open, and the pieces fly across the Church. Terrified soldier two drops his rifle and crawls under the seats. Solider three screams and tries to unlock the door. I briskly walk towards him as he struggles to escape. Finally, he turns to me and pleads for his life.

I straighten my right arm.

WOOSH!

BANG!

Another golden bullet. It hits him between the eyes as his head bursts like a firework exploding mid-air. Solider two comes out of nowhere. He's managed to pick up his rifle while I focused on soldier three. He leaps up and fires several shots. Two of them hit me! One in my left arm. One in my injured leg. I collapse down onto a seat behind me. Solider two does the same.

We both reload our weapons and plan our next move. Solider two fires a couple of warning shots up toward the ceiling. He screams at me to surrender! Solider two assures me I won't be killed if I hand myself over. While he's trying to scare and force me to surrender in the house of God, I reload my shining silver saviour. Solider two is distracted and too busy making threats and promises. I put all my weight onto the leg which hasn't been shot.

I straighten my right arm.

WOOSH!

BANG!

I drop my pistol to the ground and clutch my wounded left arm. I carefully roll up my sleeve and see a bullet sticking out of my upper arm. Blood pouring out of the hole, over my hand, and dripping onto the floor. My injured leg collapses as I'm gripping my wound in absolute agony and fall onto the solid concrete, smashing my temple on the edge of the wooden seat as I go down. I scream out in pain while lying on my side! Blood oozes from multiple holes in my body. I hear footsteps coming toward me. I lie on my back and look up toward God. I see black boots stomping with force and purpose. Next thing, a rifle is pointing in my face. It's soldier two. The golden bullet has missed him. As I scramble my brains for how the famous golden bullet could miss a shot, I see a grey cloud over me as I lose consciousness and pass out.

I slowly wake up and open my heavy eyes. I feel like I've just come out of a horrendously long sleep. One in which everything has passed me by. Everything that keeps me alive. I wonder if that's what death is. We're just closed off from all of our senses and will never get them back. Forever.

I'm inside an abandoned warehouse of horrors and can't remember the exact timeframe. It could be days, or it could have been months. It feels like I've been in an intensive coma. The room is black except for sunlight peeping through a half-rolled-up blackout blind. We've got black walls, ceiling, floor, chairs, and doors. It's the house of black. The glaring sunlight which lights up the middle of the abandoned room looks incredible, like Jesus walking tall after his resurrection. Maybe Jesus was always meant to come back to an empty, gangster-wannabee warehouse? The room stinks of dead bodies. The wounds on my arm and leg have been stitched up, by the looks of things, and wrapped up in bandages for the holes to heal. The bodily pain seems to have gone and is on the road to recovery. I can still walk, talk, move, eat, drink. There's plenty of simple foods and water. Fresh air from outside fills the room. I'm allowed to wash and clean. I've been exercising regularly to rebuild my strength and bones and gain muscle. There's a comfortable bed that folds out.

I was allowed one daytime call to check on Mrs. Sykes and Baby Owl. Until Mrs. Sykes told me to stop calling, they were both safe and still living in their beautiful cottage, which hadn't been damaged since everything was torn apart and destroyed. I could speak to Baby Owl regularly whenever she wasn't playing outside with her friends. We had bonded more than ever before. She would happily tell me about the daily mixture of friends and playful groups and the number of books she whizzed through. Baby Owl is the perfect daughter. Thanks to Mrs. Sykes, who has a kind and loving heart.

I've played my part by staying away and not infecting my family or the villages with my toxic presence and damaging past baggage. Mrs. Sykes, Baby Owl, and friends are helping the community rebuild. The villages are getting rebuilt, piece by piece, with assistance from nature and God: religion and family. The two bring about a strong connection that gives the villages a unique confidence that will help resurrect the old businesses, shops, cafes, and parks, which can all be rebuilt bigger and better than before it was destroyed and evaporated.

Bandit was like a son to me. In fact, no, Bandit was my son in heart and spirit. Biology and DNA mean absolutely nothing. It's love and emotion that makes a child. I admit that I used Bandit as a battering ram to try to take out Mr. Pyjamas. We ran to the villages and tried to warn people. Me and Bandit wanted to free Mrs. Sykes and save Baby Owl. Now, here I am. Mrs. Sykes and Baby Owl will never see me again. A handful of digital conversations is all I'm ever going have as a final goodbye.

Bandit is dead. Murdered at my feet. Mr. Pyjamas has proven that he owns my head, intelligence, life, and all of me. Mrs. Sykes and Baby Owl deserve to have a long and fulfilling life. One without me around. They must be left alone while still having money to live an extraordinary existence. That's what I'm going to give them. It's all I've ever wanted to give them. But every time, my selfish, narcissistic, power-hungry drive overtook and led everybody to where we are now. Hundreds of lives were destroyed because of me. I'm done living for my selfish desires.

My soul belongs to another and always will. I'll return to the city and do whatever is asked of me. One tortured slave is a lot better than an entire village.

I'm sitting by myself on the mattress. The breeze brings a welcoming chill that blows into my face. The passing clouds lift, and the sun shines brightly into the room. I lie down and stare at the ceiling. The room is eerily quiet.

I move over to the window and slightly pull down the blackout blind. I slowly close my eyes. All I can see is the rotting face of a bloodied Bandit and the decapitated corpse of Britain. I slap myself to eliminate the sickening images inside my head. Yet, I know deep down the vivid memories will never leave. My twisted past will forever be trapped inside my head. I'll have nightmares for the rest of my life, thanks to that evil bastard. The man who gave me 'everything I could ever ask for.' Undoubtedly, I'll be dragged into more debauchery while enslaved by the Informers.

I return to my mattress and lie, sobbing in horrific pain.

'Death is not the greatest loss in life.
The greatest loss is what dies inside us while we live.'

Mr. Pyjamas has confirmed what everybody already knows. That there's no suffering after death. Only life is suffering.

CHAPTER 13

It's the third anniversary of Bandit's death. Not a day goes by when I don't think of him. It was harrowing to see him during his final moments. I cared for his body until it was torn to pieces and sold on the market, just like I cared for my great aunt when she died of cancer. But unlike cancer, this degenerative decapitation was even more vicious. The chance to say goodbye to your loved ones is much better than a car smashing into the back of yours down the highway at night, killing you instantly. I used to ask the great aunt what was happening to her insides when she died of cancer. She couldn't tell me. All she knew was what the mainstream view of the disease was. That pretty much summed up everything, as far as I was concerned. We don't know anything about ourselves outside of the herd.

If the birth of Baby Owl was the most beautiful moment of my life, then the death of Bandit was the most horrific.

Three years on, and Mr. Pyjamas is also dead. He developed an incredibly aggressive disease that spread quickly and took him out within a few months, leaving even the most expensive private doctors bewildered about what was happening. As Mr. Pyjamas had suspected, the Informers and his Private Armies fucked off to Timbuktu, figuratively speaking. They ripped up their contracts, took as much money as possible, and even tried to kill Mr. P. I worked out deals with his workers and colleagues to stop them from murdering Mr. Pyjamas before his time. Ultimately, I sold the company and divided all of the money. I gave most of it to Mrs. Sykes, Baby Owl, and to rebuild all of the villages after their destruction. I also gave a lot of money to end the civil wars. I helped put councils and mayors in charge of the city to bring peace and order back into the metropolitan areas.

Mr. Pyjamas died in his blackened warehouse, wearing his all-black leather bikers outfit with me by his side until his last breath. He suffered during the final analysis. He could barely speak or move, struggled to eat, drink, piss, and shit without help or sleep. I had to do everything for him. I also sold Mr. Pyjamas' warehouses and kept the money for myself. It was a decent amount.

I stand over Bandit's gloomy grave as I have done every year since his death. My routine includes buying flowers and placing them on his grave. Then, I say a prayer for him and have a conversation with God. Since Bandit's death, I have only had a relationship with the Holy Father. I send Mrs. Sykes and Baby Owl digital currency, but that's it. Mrs. Sykes has moved on. She is in a new relationship with a man who Baby Owl calls 'Daddy.' They have both found the husband and father figure they never had. I've stepped back and let him take my place. The responsible, disciplined, and masculine role which I could never play. The centre of their hearts, which I could never fill. For I am nothing more than their financial provider. That's fine with me. I'll happily send them digital currency for as long as I can. They all run a cake business together, which I helped set up, and provide money whenever needed. Things are better off this way. As long as Mrs. Sykes and Baby Owl are happy, so am I. Even if it means I'm permanently erased from their lives forever.

An hour or so later, I'm sitting on the cemetery bench with a bottle of whisky. I stretch my legs out, stare at the beautiful pink sky, and watch Bandit's grave from across the cemetery. I have a couple more swigs of whisky and enjoy the burning sensation as it travels down my throat. The full moon has risen, and the pink sky has evaporated into darkness. Bright blue light shines from my phone, lighting up the bench. My surroundings remind me of Bandit. I remember when we would meet in woodland areas and car parks with minimum light to keep us focused on each other. The beauty of the stars would nearly make me cry as I'd describe the feeling to Bandit. He would be in awe of my emotions. We'd often tell each other stories from our lives. Unfortunately, these night-time events with shining technological lights often led to an argument and me being goaded into slapping or punching his face. I'd have no choice but to strike him.

Even though we were on the run, they were still some of the happiest moments of my life. Now Bandit rests in peace with Mr. Pyjamas. My relationship with Bandit and Mr. P was out of control and toxic, but they were like family to me. I'll always remember them as such. I believe in an afterlife. We will see each other someday and spend eternity with God on the spiritual plane. The physical realm doesn't mean anything to me anymore. It's merely a waiting room where we're trapped until death.

During the winter period of my life journey, I'll have completed all of my missions on Earth.

CHAPTER 14

I've just finished work. Another fourteen hours driving across the cities and villages to collect or drop off whatever's required. I have a website set up, so by the time I've pulled out my mattress and already got all my bookings for the following day, I can get some sleep before waking up around 4:00am for a full day of removals, usually finishing up around 7:00pm.

Then, I come home and eat whatever I've got in the cupboard, usually a soup of some kind, hot or cold, I'm not arsed. After that, I'll set up everything for going to sleep, and then I'll likely read something on the internet until I pass out from exhaustion. Usually, some conspiracy theory about wars and invasions that could occur within the next few months. I highly doubt it, but I read it anyway. Things have been very peaceful within the cities and villages for years, so there's no need to worry about violent breakouts or ongoing social conflicts.

I don't have any friends, family, or a boss. I'm not keen on either. Been there and done that. Nothing but trouble. I spend all of my spare time alone and prefer it that way. Honestly, I don't have much spare time when I choose to work seven days per week. The only time I have outside of removals are these hours between drinking soup, sleeping, and waking up. I could afford to live in better conditions than I do. I've tried in the past, and it wasn't significant. None of it matters. Keep it simple, stupid. A one-room flat is all I need nowadays. My rent is cheap and I pay a bloke whose office I help empty. This landlord is doing very dodgy dealings. As an ex-scumbag criminal myself, I don't judge or even question. Just do away with his evil deeds and take any evidence wherever he needs me to. He owns a few properties and rents this hole to me for nothing.

There's a medium-sized mattress with brown and yellow stains. I use my workbag as a pillow and sheets for warmth. I also have sheets hanging over my window to keep the light out. I hate the sun and night-time street lamps.

I've got wooden cupboards with sturdy handles, staying on as you'd expect. There's a working fridge, sink with fresh running water, jars I use as glasses, bowls, plates, knives, forks, and working electricity. I also have a small toilet for my brown shits and yellow pisses. I'd live out of my big, white van if I wanted. Considering what I'd realistically be content with, this tiny flat is a luxury. But I've decided to sleep in a more secure place than a van.

My sex life isn't as bad as you'd expect. I often get invited into the gaffs of Milfs and Gilfs. Their husbands, children, or grandchildren will be away somewhere and I'll end up shagging these middle-aged tarts or very old granny's. Between the ages of forty to seventy. The eldest woman I've fucked was seventy-nine years old! The most boring shag was the youngest and most attractive. She was forty years old and acted like I owed her something. She just lied on her back and made no effort whatsoever. She kept asking me to finish up during the act as her husband would return soon. Boring.

I'm not invited in for sex that often. Maybe once every three or four months. It's never by the same woman. Sometimes I think they've booked a removal just for a quick fuck! When I get there the item they've booked to be removed is something they could have quickly taken themselves. Something as simple as a tiny table.

I don't remotely bother with current events or political movements. The cities are run democratically, very corrupt, and all about money, but your vote still allegedly matters. I guess it's better than the days during the civil wars when the cities were shattered. Nobody thought they would ever come back. Never mind thriving hubs of entertainment. I like to think I had something to do with that by giving my inheritance and earnings away to rebuild communities and businesses. The village is still an absolute paradise. A place where you can go for multiple walks a day in nature, swim in the lakes, and read books underneath apple trees in the park. Pubs for piss ups, coffee shops for a catch up, and restaurants for families.

Last time I checked, it's still where Mrs. Sykes and Baby Owl live. I've not seen either of them for at least three years. I last saw Mrs. Sykes and Baby Owl at her birthday party. Not only did she not know who I was, but she didn't attempt to speak to me. Mrs. Sykes made no effort to get me and Baby Owl to interact. I don't know why she invited me. Probably to show me how happy she was without me. How much of a better husband she had found. How much of a better father Baby Owl had. That was it for me from that point. I stopped sending them monthly digital currency as they had a new man in their life to look after them and see to their existence. I wished Mrs. Sykes the best and told Baby Owl I loved her. That was the end of our relationship.

I'm an addict and always will be. But only booze nowadays. A bottle of whisky every day sees me through. Half in the morning when I wake up and half at night before sleep. I'm so used to the whisky that I can barely feel its effects. A part from waking me up for a hard day's graft and knocking me out for a hefty sleep. Its main product is keeping my mental issues inside their boxes. I've tried to give up whisky several times and woke up in hospital for attempting suicide.

Some little cunt always finds and saves me. Whether it's my dodgy landlord coming around for a favour and catching me as I'm about to hang myself with my black leather belt. Or I somehow wake up in a hospital having my stomach pumped, even getting rescued from jumping off a building. I like to think it was God saving me each time. My time clearly isn't over. God has more for me to do. I highly doubt I'll ever do anything with my life again, but it's not mine to end whenever I want. He saved me for a reason. Until God was ready to take me, so with that in mind, I returned to a bottle of whisky each day. It ironically keeps me from suicide or having a mental breakdown.

With everything I've been through, this is the life I've chosen for myself. I do enough to get by and just wait for the grave. Hopefully, I'll pass away sooner rather than later. But knowing my luck, I'll still be doing removals, sleeping on mattresses, and drinking whisky until I die.

End